The goal of this book is to take a second step towards something I am passionate about. This book you're holding is an idea of mine turned into words, coloured with various emotions. The various short stories will make you laugh (at times), allow you to indulge and enjoy strong relationships, which is something I truly believe in, and will also make you cry at times.

The stories are unique in their own ways. When a child is born, we never inculcate just one theme or a genre to follow, instead we let him feel different feelings and gestures, keeping the same thing in mind this book is my child with different thoughts turned into short stories.

So is life. Life has a lot of incidents, some we feel, and some we just remember till our last breath.

JASHN
An Awakening

GEETIKA K. BAKSHI

Inkfeathers Publishing
www.inkfeathers.com

Jashn – An Awakening
Written by Geetika K. Bakshi
Paperback Edition

First Published in India in 2022
by Inkfeathers Publishing, New Delhi 110095

Copyright © Geetika K. Bakshi 2022

www.inkfeathers.com

Life is a lot of happiness entwined with eerie wonder,
love, hunger, and defeat. To evolve as a whole,
we must take a sip of each flavour.

- Geetika K. Bakshi

CONTENTS

FOREWORD

From as long as I can remember, short stories have always intrigued me. They reveal as much as they conceal. They pull you into the world created as much as they leave certain elements to your imagination. It is like savouring a small box of chocolates which may get over fast, but the aftertaste lingers long after it melts into the mouth. In Jashn – An Awakening, Geetika K. Bakshi has packed more in less in each of the twenty stories that are a part of this beautiful anthology of heartfelt tales. She holds the reader's hands and takes us through a myriad of emotions that we experience in our daily lives. Love, trust, betrayal, pain, acceptance, and joy – it is all there in generous doses.

Isn't it true that life is synonymous with stories? Stories are all around us. Stories are within us. Stories are those gems from our lives which when stringed together give us a sparkling and satisfying vision of our life's journeys. It is this very essence of life that has been encapsulated by Geetika into her stories. Just like life, each story gives as a glimpse of a different feeling and relationship dynamics. From smiling through your tears to being shocked at an unexpected turn in the narrative to feeling heartbroken due to an unfortunate situation, the reader is bound to connect to the highs, lows, and everything in between.

Geetika has an unassuming style of narration which fits in seamlessly with the genre of the book. She also touches upon social themes without making it pronounced and subtly makes a point about gender inequality and biases in the society. The characters in the stories are people we see everywhere. In some, you will also find your reflection. Maybe, these characters will also take you back to some long-lost relationships, or they might make you relook at some of your choices.

The strength of a short story lies in the balance it strikes between completeness and incompleteness. This anthology does that with its brevity and breezy undertone. So, pick up that cup of coffee (or whatever is your drink of the day) and delve right into the pages ahead for a wholesome, contented reading experience!

Anupama Dalmia

Blogger, Author and

Serial entrepreneur

One

THE LOST EARRING

A lot of people say that a woman will survive after her husband dies as long as she acknowledges her commitments. She is wise enough to recognise the practicality of life and to mourn his death in silence. Lalit lived far too long as a widower but far too short as a married man. He married at the age of twenty-seven. Marriage presented him with several privileges, in addition to his status, but he never found his soul mate.

He had a son and a daughter during his ten-year marriage to Anupama. They seemed to have no affection for each other. He met Anupama through a family arrangement and married her without even getting to know her. They achieved all of their family's goals, but they never found solace in each other. Lalit always admired Anupama for the way she managed their family and children. Anupama, who was still preoccupied with her own little universe, never had high hopes from him either. She did a lot of things to surprise their children, but nothing special for Lalit.

On their tenth anniversary, Lalit decided to commemorate a decade of marriage by visiting a Swarovski jewellery store and purchasing rose-gold danglers for his wife. He paid for it, but was unaware of the delicacy, just like he was about their marriage. In his enthusiasm, just as he was about to leave the shop, a lady barged into him; the earrings slipped and a few gems fell out, forming a very obvious shape of an "L". The lady vanished with such lightning speed that he could only see a giant mole on her left arm.

He asked the salesgirl to change it, but she refused, saying, "You bought it, sir."

He agreed to send Anupama the same earring. Just then, the lady returned to the shop with a tiny kitten and sighed, "She might have died if I hadn't hurried! I apologise for the inconvenience. I'll take these earrings and repair them later. You are welcome to take another." offered the lady. To his ears, her words sounded like music. He seemed to be lost in her voice, as if a romantic song was playing in the background.

"No, it's fine! I'm going to get another one. You don't have to pay." he politely denied.

"The letter 'L' stands for life, but also 'love,'" she explained as she observed the fallen gems.

"'L' stands for life, love, and Lalit," exclaimed Lalit, but not too loudly.

She seemed perplexed. "So, please accept my apologies."

Nothing, Lalit cut to the chase and moved towards the counter.

The lady seemed to be in her mid-thirties and looked unmarried, but it would be horrifying if Lalit dared to ask her any of this. She appeared to be a loved yet complicated person.

"Mumma, hurry up. I'm running late for my party! That piece of jewel, you can get it later."

Lalit's wacky imagination had gone awry. He went back to the cash register to get another pair. He reasoned that Anupama would appreciate the gesture.

After the purchase, he got into his car and headed around. They lived in a multi-storey house. He had a special affection for his aunt, Radha, his father's elder brother's wife. She teased him, saying it would be the first gift in years. For the first time, he blushed. Over the years of alienation in marriage, he might have fallen in love with Anupama. Anupama had not come down since that morning, according to Radha, and there had been a lot of coughing all day.

****

"Okay, *Ji*, let's meet on Saturday. It's Ajay's day off from work, and Nidhi will be at home as well. If all works out, who knows if the phone conversation will create a new bond between the families."

"Archana *Ji*, without a doubt!"

Lalit hung up the phone and turned to Nidhi, saying, "The family seems decent. Let's get together on Saturday."

Nidhi blushed. She adored Ajay, and for her dad, the background didn't matter, or so she assumed. Nidhi has no recollection of her father as a husband. She just knew him as a good man and a fantastic father.

****

Saturday, around 4 p.m., they met at Starbucks.

Nidhi was nervous to introduce her father to Ajay's mother.

Archana seemed to have a nice personality. A lovable mother-in-law, any father would want for her daughter. Something about that lady was fascinating, though; her smile, her eyes, her jawline – even at the age of 50, she was well maintained.

Lalit's thoughts have gone to the dogs as she chuckled silently.

"You both can go out and talk."

"Sure, Papa," muttered Nidhi.

Whenever Lalit talked to Ajay's mom about Ajay or their family background, his eyes kept shifting to something. He was bewildered to see the rose-gold earrings juggling in Ajay's mother's ears. One earring had the initial letter "L." 'L' for life. 'L' for Lalit. She also had a mole on her arm. He was left spellbound that this was the same lady who had barged into him years ago. Today, she was the "would-be-mother-in-law" to his daughter.

"That earring?" asked Lalit.

"Yeah, what's the matter?" Archana asked back.

"I bought the same pair years ago for my wife. It had the same initials."

Embarrassed, she asked, "What initials?"

"'L' for life, 'L' for love."

"Oh! I can't believe it. Are you the same person?"

"Yes. Such a small world."

Just then, Nidhi and Ajay came in, both angry.

"Let's leave, Ma!" Ajay said.

"What happened?" Archana asked, bewildered.

"I said, let's just leave! I don't want to stay here anymore. I don't think I am here for any further explanation!"

"I didn't ask for any!" retorted Nidhi in defence. "You don't even have the patience to understand what I wanted to say. You assumed something else and got furious. I just suggested that we spend some time together before committing for a lifetime."

"What do you mean by that? Do you want a live-in?"

"I never said that! What if after marriage, we feel like aliens to each other?"

"Oh, so every couple stays together before getting hitched?"

"By together, I meant, we should ask for some time from our parents. I am not in a hurry to get married."

"Whatever, Nidhi. The discussion is over."

"Ajay, what is wrong with her idea?" interfered Archana. "Do you know why I never got married? I never thought that someday, my son would talk someday like a patriarch. I believed you to be the producer, not the prisoner of society. She meant that she wants to know you before saying yes for a lifetime."

****

"Hahaha, you never told me that you have an impression on your heart?"

"How could I?"

"That was such a teeny meet by chance. I just got a good feeling about those earrings, and also, they are beyond doubt a lucky charm for me. I always wear them to any important meeting. Tell me, did your wife like the other ones you bought that day?"

"I hope she did. It was our 10th anniversary. We had not felt any connection in 10 years. We just lived under one roof as complete strangers. We made out, had kids, still like we did not know each other. It was too complicated. Anupama had been always busy with her chores. Never complained about anything. The day I wanted to felicitate her was the day I found her dead. I never knew of her illness. It was a journey I didn't know when it started and ended."

"Why didn't you marry someone? You are a pandora of positivity, attitude, and class."

That had been the problem with Lalit.

She continued, "I have seen an image of the man I used to hate in my son. I adopted him and raised him single-handedly to prove I never need a man to have and raise a child, but for love. Only for love! No one understood. Neither then, nor now. Look at you. You were trapped in an alienated marriage, but never thought of finding love because before you could find love, you were taken."

"Will you marry me?"

"What? Are you mad? I am fifty!"

"And I am fifty-seven. What's the big deal?"

"I loved you at first sight and want to love you till my last breath. Will you let me surrender to you, my destiny? 'L' for love, 'L' for Life, 'L' for Lalit?"

****

The marriage was solemnised.

"Today, Mom and Dad. Next week, it's us. Isn't it too complicated?" Nidhi asked Ajay.

"It won't be, *Jaan*."

Two

THE EIGHT VOW

Aisha

"Hey! You are the one who can conquer the world and set an example for many, and this is nothing but a viva test."

"You know, Shubham, how much I hate science. I don't want to learn about the iodine effect on a leaf, and if it turns black or red like my period stains."

"Wait, I'll help you. It is just four steps you need to remember. Majorly, it is boiling the leaf normally, and then in ethanol for a few minutes. Then wash with water and spread onto a white tile. Add iodine solution from a dropping pipette. After a few minutes, the parts of the leaf that contain starch turn blue-black which confirms that it has starch."

It was the first time you appeared in front of me. I have been always neither an atheist nor a theist because I believed there was some power behind us to support us. I'm a believer who denies worshiping lords but preaches that soft voice who always guides me: your voice. I am never convinced in praying to the Lord in the form of stones and adorned with heavy jewellery.

Since then, I always found you with me, be it saving me from dad's scolding or mom's beating behind the clipped doors.

You have always been the man of my dreams. Since the day you came in front of me again, years later, when I was just 21, graduated from IIM, and just like every young person, I dreamt of my own start-up. You always gave me ears to listen to my everyday changing plans and then put your baffling ideas.

I never forgot the day you stopped your car on my way, just because minutes ago, I was driving rashly and was about to bang into yours. It was meant to start our love story. I was angry at you for stopping your car that way, but then once you opened your mouth to utter, "Are you crazy? Does the road belong to your father?" Those two questions of yours swept away all my anger. The man who used to speak with me all the time was in front of me today.

Just like his voice, he is smart and handsome too.

You indeed gave a long lecture, but I missed everything, and concentrated on your eyebrows, your lips, the lines on your forehead. Your eyebrows seem freshly plucked. You must be somewhere between 24-25 years. A perfect match. Just then, a frequent click of fingers. Click, click, click! I stood there in embarrassment. All I could have said was sorry and dropped my card, which had my new start-up details and my phone number, on the windshield of your car.

I drove to the United coffee house, and for the first time, the voice behind me had a face to guide me. What to do next? I wondered, and he uttered to wait and enjoy my life and plan the business's first step. I had a meeting at the coffee shop, which went in vain as the investor didn't seem to be impressed. Just then, Shubham said, "You need to be, rejected many times to be successful one day."

And I felt like you came in-person to wipe my tears. Indeed, you did, as just then I saw my phone ringing. True caller reflected the name 'Shubham Chaturvedi.' I picked up and it was you.

"Hello, am I talking to Aisha?"

"Oh yes. This is Aisha."

"Are you into marketing management?"

"Yes, sir. May I know who this is?"

"This is the one who shouted at you this morning. I called you, certainly not to be sorry as I only apologise when it's my mistake."

"Oh please. It's okay. How may I help you?" I tried sounding a little stunned to receive this call as if I were not expecting it.

"I need to fix up a meeting with you as soon as possible. I need someone who can market my dream business, sorry, my wife's dream business, to every possible corner of this world. She was living only for her dream 'Paridhan textiles.'"

My jaw dropped, knowing that you were married. I felt like I was ripped in a go. Everything I had washed away from my hands just like that.

Shit. This can't happen. The voice belongs to me. It has been guiding me since always. Many times, you confessed your love to me. Then how can it belong to someone else?

"Hello. Hello! Are you listening?"

"Yes, Mr. Shubham. I am here. I can come. Kindly draft a mail for what you desire in the project. Then drop a text of the address, day, and time. I'll get back to you."

"Sure. May you understand how my dead wife's dream is important to me."

"Yes. Certainly, sir."

The call was disconnected.

What? Did he just say, 'dead wife'?

Means she is no more.

First time ever in my life, I felt relaxed at someone's pain. Is this what a sense of achievement feels like? I never knew that. Whatever it was, it was the sense of utter peace that night.

I got an email the same evening, followed by a text message saying the next meeting will be on Friday at 2 pm at Café Tesu. Oh my god, this man knows me to every extent without even knowing me at all, or these are just the similarities we share.

You just said café Tesu. My favourite place. I zapped the channel and enjoyed two movies at a time. How relaxed I was to meet the love of my life. This time work is not the priority. From this meeting onwards, my days and nights are nothing faster than waxing and waning of the moon. Each time my all efforts were to look the best I could.

A year passed, then the second, and you are now an owner of Paridhan textiles — India's fastest-growing textile brand. Today is the celebration of 'our' joint venture. Yes, 'our' joint venture!

I took out my best red dress for the award ceremony. I wanted to look the best tonight because I know how special this night is.

We both had a lot of fun and appreciation as we were the youngest achievers at the event.

"I've to go to the loo."

"Sure, darling. I'll wait for you in the car."

"Ok!"

Ten minutes later was the best moment of my life when I saw Shubham propose to me with a diamond solitaire in his hand, and he was on his knees.

I was on cloud nine tonight. Of course, I have been waiting for this day all my life.

****

She said yes, and even Shubham's parents were happy to have Aisha as their daughter-in-law. They always wanted Shubham to move on in his life, because when he lost Maira, he just stepped into serene youth.

Soon they both were to start the journey of their life together. Dates were fixed, and a quarter later, the D-day came. They both tied a knot, Shubham adorned Aisha's head with red vermilion, and they took seven auspicious vows.

The only thing was different that Shubham took seven, but Aisha took eight. That it was all a trap. A trap she set to have Shubham in her life. That Aisha was the same ugly junior from school who used to look at Shubham from behind the pillars. She even remembers Shubham making love to Maira, the head girl of our school, as they both were madly in love. She was broken when she got to know Shubham and Maira were tying the wedlock.

She first worked on herself and then laid a trap to kill Maira. Aisha smartly spent days planning Maira's death. That was the night of Shubham and Maira's first wedding anniversary when she was found dead in the bathtub full of roses, which she decorated for her husband.

With each step, a movie was playing at the back of her head. The bell of room service, handing over the bubble bath to Maira. That it was her in disguise in black and white staff attire. The bubble bath had the sweet fragrance of Lavender. Along with that, the complimentary juice she gave her had castor oil seeds.

They both were each other's from now on and share all the darkest secrets except the eighth vow. She had a winning smile on her face.

Three

THE SWIRLS IN LOVE

"Shobhna, you can do it. You can do it. It's easy, darling. Just push. Push… Push… Push…"

"Shut up, Ashish! You be here in my place and push by yourself. I told you earlier not to put all your stuff in that suitcase, but you never listen to me. It's been two years since we tied the knot, and now, I'm yours forever mistake corrector."

"If I hadn't had this slipped disc, I would have pushed this box by myself. Then you would be surprised to see that 'Shaktimaan' in your loving husband."

"I remember you did the same thing when we were to catch our flight for our first national trip together to Assam. I understand you loved Assam very much, but since we came back from our honeymoon, you haven't taken a single sign to plan a trip to this destination. I'll tell you in detail why I wanted to travel to this place so badly. First, you answer my question and dare you change the topic. That time I told you not to take such a gigantic giant suitcase, but you are a Mr. Model since always. You need matching shoes and even matching scarves. You are worse than a girl. That security check at the airport didn't allow it, and we ended up missing our flight."

"What should I have done? The beautiful spots need to be clicked with perfect attire. And signs? Really?"

"Haan, toh mera ye cheesy tumhare cheesy part se better tha (My being cheesy was better than your being cheesy)."

"Remember when you went to, your mom's place to stay some nights. I was enjoying being a bachelor on my bed to the core. Enjoying Netflix and chills with Red Bull and Nachos. Then you posted a love letter to my office. The next morning, I reached the office, and Raj- my office boy- handed, it over saying, *"Bhaiya, Bhabhi ka khat aaya hai* (Brother, your wife has sent you a letter)." I was a little embarrassed, but I enjoyed reading it for sure. It came along with my favourite Chinese Hakka noodles you cooked for me."

"Haan, don't forget that a love letter of mine also had a beautiful thing attached to it."

"Oh hell, yes. How can I forget that? A credit card statement, as you always wanted me to come with you for shopping. The more I denied, you found your way to make me part of your crazy shopping trips."

"You remember when you called me specially, making me nervous? When I returned, you showed me the black lacy dress and lingerie that you bought to make me crazy for you. I was enjoying beer with my friends, and you could have held your excitement for two more hours and ended up calling me that you had a migraine and wanted to see the doctor as soon as possible. Mom and Dad were out of town, so how could you have let go this opportunity? And it was nothing less than Samantha in Sex and the city 2."

"Oh, and the time when you ordered me to give you love bites so you could happily flaunt it in the office to your female friends and would call my chest, your field."

"Ha-ha-ha, that was awesome. Oh, my god. You can't be this imaginative, Shobhna. I mean, look at your name. Seems like a typical *Bhartiya Naari* (Indian woman), whose sole purpose is to make her husband happy."

"Oh, this was also to make my husband happy. We kept both of us in pleasure mode, always," winked Shobhna.

Shobhna took a deep breath, and Ashish laid his hand on her head. There was a hustle and sound of the machine. Dripping of glucose was audible, even in all that chaos. She smiled, and he remembered her tantrums as a newly married girl.

Him not being Punjabi, his mom didn't allow her to wear fake jewellery for one year. She still had *Chooda* (Punjabi jewellery for newlywed) as a prerequisite to make up for being Punjabi. She moved mountains to keep this accessory on for a year. Every night he was irritated, but her concern was to shine with that *Chooda* every morning. Summers were all about vexed wrists and arms, but she used talcum powder and a hair dryer to let skin under it dry.

The clock struck twelve in the hospital room as it had in the past four days. With its melodious tune, it notified that it was midnight. Ashish, along with his in-laws, parents, and Shobhna's brother, started singing a happy anniversary song to her. It was their 4th wedding anniversary.

"At this moment, I am infinite, yet I am angry at myself for taking your doubt for granted," uttered Ashish.

"Three months ago, when you told me about Karan, the guy who stalked you during college. He ran into you in Ambience mall when you were shopping all alone. He stepped in front of you and started asking you how I was. Was I taking care of you or not? Why did you go shopping alone? That day when you came home, I was busy on my X-box. I am really sorry. I ignored you when you said that three days in a row, he met you at some or the other place, pretending as if it were a coincidence. Karan might have noticed you more than your own husband. I wish I had given you my shoulder that time, so today, you would be wrapped in my arms in love and not in the rest. I literally never felt this bad in my life, not even when I failed in my CA exams and had settled for this NGO job."

"Mr. Ashish, you have to be a little courageous, and I need to have a talk in person with you for a while," requested Dr. Dutta. This case was in the headlines of all renowned newspapers and all TV channels. Karan had eloped, and the police were after him.

****

"May I come in?" Ashish asked from behind the door of Dr. Dutta's cabin.

"Yes, please, have a seat. Ashish, you are a very nice, supportive, and liberal husband. This is what I know about you, being Shobhna's doctor. She would always talk about you. I saw you for the first time when she had a miscarriage last to last year. We both consoled her that it happens quite often. Now, there is no need to worry, but there is bad news. This rape case uncovers a big loss for both of you. Her soul will be treated by you, but her body, I doubt!" Dr. Dutta paused. "Four days ago, she was brought into this nursing home for the second time. She met with me that morning and was very happy to know that she was three months pregnant. She was on cloud nine that the treatment finally bore fruit.

While Ashish was processing everything, Dr. Dutta continued. "Unfortunately, she may not ever conceive now. Due to this rape, she not only had bruises all over her body, but also lost her baby. She will not be able to bear a child again, certainly not in the near future."

Mid-conversation, a sister barged into Dr. Dutta's cabin, saying that Shobhna had gained consciousness and was looking for Ashish.

****

Shobna was doing well within the next few months. Karan was also behind bars under lifetime imprisonment. Both Shobhna and Ashish decided to adopt a boy. They both wanted a girl, but the orphanage had some issues with them. They denied them a girl child. Yet they were both happy with 'Rhythm.'

****

Four years had passed, and it was Rhythm's 4th birthday party tonight. All of a sudden, Shobhna shouted from inside her room. As everybody came to her rescue, she said that it was a miracle. The mail said she was pregnant. It was a one in a million kind of miracle.

****

The happy family of four lived in fast-paced Mumbai city, where Ashish brought Shobhna after that tragedy. Ashish, Shobhna, Rhythm, and Kiarika; all lived, loved, and laughed together. Ashish changed a lot. He became more sensible to take care of the queen and the princess of his life.

Four

THE LAST THING I EXPECTED-
DARKER THAN THE BLACK

"Lost again, you fool! You never listen to me. You are always like that. Don't you dare call yourself my best friend again."

"I'm sorry, Shelly. I know you must have shared something very serious which I missed."

"Oh really? But my stuff can never be important for you. You carry on with your thoughtful world," snapped Shelly.

Once again, Riddhima stood alone, just with her isolation. She stepped towards her favourite place. Though from inside, she was angry with herself as always.

You know Shelly's problem so well. How can you do this to her? She thought to herself.

Your own job hardly permits you to extend your long weekend. Look at her job. She will fly to Berlin next month, and last month she visited Mauritius and Maldives, her subconscious answered.

She questioned herself, does your friend think the same way as you? About how many problems you have? Despite everything, you are always there to hear her problems.

The answer was the same as always, *I don't care if she doesn't. I do, and that's enough. I care for her, and I know she does, too.*

****

Finally, the day when Shelly was getting hitched had come. An independent woman was going to be someone's wife tomorrow morning. All preparations had been through.

I know she is not happy, but we are Indians, and a woman who has said yes to a 'Rishta' can't say no now – otherwise, log kya kahenge? (what will people say?)

Riddhima, who was there in every single decision of Shelly's life, now repented the cruel circumstances that she wasn't there with her at that time.

"That's the best thing about life. Experiences teach us how to hold on."

Riddhima hadn't yet told Shelly that she was going to Old Manali the next day. She knew very well that Shelly would kill her once she knew that she was going alone, that too, on a bike. She had borrowed a bullet from a friend and had decided to leave the day after Shelly's wedding.

She was upset that she left her job without having another one in hand, relying on a person she hardly knew but was madly in love with. A friend whom she met a few months ago at her favourite place. They became very close friends in a short span. She loved him dearly, but at the same time, she had to accept the fact they could never be together. He taught her how to live in the present. In the time they spent together, he would read her writings and motivate her by telling her that she deserved much better than what she was doing today.

Benefitting the time she now had, she started the bike and drove to Manali. It wasn't that easy to reach there all alone, but as it was said, "To reach somewhere, you need to start somewhere, and it is only the start which needs courage." Riddhima had borne a lot of scars till now, but she refused to surrender, and ate the pies of life with a smile.

She made local connections whenever she stopped to have a sip of tea or for food. She clicked pictures with localities. First time ever in her life, she felt so light. All the way to old Manali, she became a free bird, the thing she had always dreamt of. She looked at her inked hand, elated that she was justifying her tattoos.

Two days passed that way. While she was enjoying her beer, she heard a similar laugh. A laugh that let her heart beat a little faster. She looked around but couldn't see anyone. Once again, the same laugh echoed, followed by a name she thought the laugh belonged to.

"Neel!" someone said.

She stood up and gaited towards the table where he was sitting. They both exchanged smiles. The last thing she expected was that her first solo trip would take her to her love. He was the same person she used to be with in the evenings.

"You're here, Riddhima. Hi!"

"Hi. So, you are here with your friends?"

"Yeah. As always, a sudden plan. Where are your friends?"

"I have come alone."

"What?"

"Yes."

"How?"

"On a bullet."

"Are you crazy?"

"Like hell," she said and laughed.

"Where are you staying?"

"Snow valley resorts."

"Such a small world. We three are also there for three days. When are you leaving?"

"I don't know."

"What?"

"Yes, Neel. I'll leave when I feel like."

"What about your office?"

"I left my job before coming here. Someone suggested that it's not my cup of tea."

Both of them laughed, and they understood that the universe was planning something.

"Hey, do one thing. Join us in the evening for a barbecue."

"Aah, sounds good. Sure."

****

She opened the bottle of wine. Neel and his friends were high on Old Monk. A chit-chat session was going on.

"I never knew you cook so well."

Time passed, and it was 2 a.m. now. Neel's friends were tired and went to sleep, but both of them still had a lot to talk about. Riddhima moved towards the balcony, and Neel followed her.

There was a moment of silence. The next moment, Riddhima kissed Neel, and he felt a bit uncomfortable.

"What was that?"

"As if you don't know!"

This time, Neel came forward, and they kissed, but it wasn't a firm one.

After their kiss, she whispered a bye, but before she could move, he asked her to join them for Solang valley the next day.

She said she was there on a solo trip, and if they were meant to be, they would meet there.

They both went to their respective rooms and slept with smiles on their faces.

Early morning, she started her bike. Neel heard the sound, and it worked as a wake-up alarm. She was on a platform covered with snow, and suddenly, a snowball hit her. She wasn't surprised to see him standing behind. Her happiness knew no bounds, as somewhere, she also wanted him to come.

Even Neel's friends found Riddhima a cheerful person. A bowl of Maggie added spice to their talks.

"I'm leaving tomorrow morning," said Riddhima.

"What? You were supposed to be here for a few more days."

"Yes, I was. But I guess one should leave the place they like the most. Otherwise, there is a fear of falling in love, and it hurts as it's one-sided because 'hills are hills they cannot love us back.'"

They had dinner together, just them, as the other two friends left them alone.

They didn't talk much. The silence was the winner. In the end, she thanked Neel.

"Why?"

"You will find your answer soon."

The next morning, she started her bike and left the place without looking back.

While driving back, she thought how some people left an impression darker than black yet allowed you to see through it.

****

Five

THE RED POUCH AND THE GUILTY CONSCIENCE

Take it.

No, the other part of her mind consoled.

You'll need it. There were silent chatters in her mind.

Wait! What no! Why would I need a glass paediatric tube? I'm here for the blood sample, just give it and move, she questioned her subconscious.

Though her mind was constantly telling her that it was of no use, she still couldn't resist sliding two tubes in her pockets. She needs it, or not, that would be decided later. With time her urge to steal things unnecessarily had swollen up with guilt. Sometimes she found herself cursing for not controlling her gluttony in the eyes. She failed to understand why she still shoplifted such petty things when she was now well settled and could easily afford such stuff.

Like this morning she ended up slipping test tubes.

What would you do with this? She asked herself.

"Kleptomaniac you are," uttered Narayani. "Have you ever even thought about how clumsy the habit is?"

Shubhavi made a blended face while ambulating towards the counter to place an order for two cappuccinos.

Since there were a lot of people, she started checking out new coffee flavours. She lifted a packet and looked here and there. Everyone was busy having coffee, chatting, smoking, and reading. Her eyes ushered wall to wall and she slipped the packet into her bag.

She placed the order, and they had coffee. While going back in the car, Shubhavi told Narayani about her action.

"Stop the car!"

When she didn't, Narayani shouted again, "I said stop now. I don't want to ride back in your car. No matter what, you are supposed to steal things as if this is your job. Why on earth did I choose to be a friend of a thief?

"I am no thief. I am just a victim of the social recession," uttered Shubhavi.

"Ha-ha. Hilarious. For you! For me, it's conspicuous. I mean, you have everything, still, I find you stealing every now and then. I feel pity for you, Shubhavi," Narayani took her complete name in ages.

"Don't get angry. I promise I'll work on it. I'll try not to do it again."

"Why don't you go to a counsellor?"

"Ha-ha. In our society, alcoholism, and drug addiction are treated as an illness and people could get counselling. But if I tell anyone about my thing, I'll be judged in every aspect. Some people might check calendars to check the date to match my visit and a petty or huge theft happened at their places," exclaimed Shubhavi. Do you want to check? Go home and tell your mom about my problem."

"Come sit by me. Have you ever thought about why on earth you do this?"

"I have been racking my brain after each incident. What I know is the pleasure I get. This habit is increasing now, and I'm loving it."

"Shut up!" Narayani left her at this.

****

It had been almost six months since Narayani had not talked to Shubhavi. Shubhavi did not have many friends, just acquaintances.

The best part about Narayani was that she did not tell anyone the reason for the silence between the two friends. Deep down, Narayani still believed that they were friends, and that she was just punishing Shubhavi for her deeds.

She tried to contact her for the umpteenth time, but there was no response.

She sat with hands her against her forehead, and just then, there was a flash on her screen. It was Narayani. She had called her for a coffee.

"Yes, I know I'll receive such baffled expressions. I really want to meet you to share some good news," Narayani said.

"Are you prego?"

"Shut your dustbin mouth."

"Without marriage, huh? So, are you getting married?"

Shubhavi could feel Narayani turning cherry over the call.

"Woohoo, woohoo! My bestie is getting married. You will be delighted to know that I have also changed. This is why I was calling, to get you back."

"Double celebration. See you at six at Barista."

"Hmm."

****

"Tujhe yaad na meri aayi, kisi se ab kya kehna," Shubhavi teased Narayani for not remembering her during the groom hunt.

"No, *baba*. I was just angry with you," Narayani muttered and suddenly felt twitchy and restless. A man was hovering in the background, continuously peering at them.

"Let's go, Shubhavi. I am not feeling good. Let's go home."

"Why?" questioned Shubhavi.

"That man is making me uncomfortable."

"Such morons are everywhere. He doesn't have the balls to do anything."

"Still, let's go. Please."

"Okay."

They left the place, but the man was still following them. Both were worried. With each step, he kept coming closer. Shubhavi decided to stop even after Narayani's cautious remarks.

"What is your problem?"

"Pouch."

"Huh?"

"Pouch. I need my pouch."

"Which pouch?"

"The red one."

"Huh," she made a strange face, signing that she was perplexed. He seemed too high on cocaine or something.

"Pouch… pouch… now… pouch…"

She moved towards the metro gate, but suddenly felt something sharp on her tummy. She was stunned to see it was a knife wrapped in a cloth.

"If you shout, the knife wouldn't budge from your stomach."

Seeing this, Narayani started crying. She tried to move in order to save her friend, but there were three more guys surrounding her.

"Give the pouch and go. We don't want you."

"Which pouch?"

"The red pouch. In the local market. You picked it up when I dropped it."

"Yeah, I picked it because you dropped it. I liked the pouch, and that's not even theft. Moreover, I don't even know where it is."

"Shut up. The pouch is expensive."

"Ha-ha," she laughed out loud and talked in gibberish. "The pouch was too shoddy."

"Shut up!"

Seeing that Shubhavi wasn't taking them seriously, they attacked Narayani. One of the three shot her twice in the chest.

"No! Idiot! Who asked you to do that?"

"You impulsive…" cried the man that had attacked Shubhavi. In a jiff, they ran away.

People gathered around, but no one came forward to succour. Finally, she managed to stop a car, and they took her to the hospital. Narayani muttered to Shubhavi, "I was wrong to accept you have changed."

Shubhavi, in distress, consoled her as she slipped into a lifetime of guilt.

****

Narayani's ashes were drowned in the Ganges as per the Hindu ritual. Shubhavi was in her room, tears rolling down her cheeks. She gathered courage and opened the trousseau where she kept 'The red pouch' that she hadn't touched since she picked it up. She emptied it, jerked it, and only a few coins dropped on the bed. She threw it, wondering why that boy was asking for the pouch.

It still felt swollen. She picked it up, and with all her efforts, she almost tore it. She was bewildered to see seven diamonds, crystal clear diamonds, in there.

"These boys will not leave this or me. I lost Narayani to these. They might be coming after me," uttered Shubhavi in whispers. She cried to apologise that she mustn't have picked it up in the first place.

The shame and burden of being caught as a shoplifter cannot be erased ever; never, people will become hawk around you throughout life.

Six

LET ME SAY I LOVE YOU

The Ketchup song was playing as loud as possible.

Aserejé, ja deje tejebe tude jebere

Sebiunouba majabi an de bugui an de buididipí

Aserejé, ja deje tejebe tude jebere

Sebiunouba majabi an de bugui an de buididipí

Aserejé, ja deje tejebe tude jebere

Sebiunouba majabi an de bugui an de buididipí

Rachit and Vishwas were dancing in the lobby area as both were drunk. There were only two flats, and moreover, the neighbour was out. It was a celebration day. Vishwas's first love story was a great success.

Not being a booze hound, they both were high today. God knows it was happiness, or they really are too drunk. They were dancing, hooting, and whatnot. They were copying the staple steps of their childhood famous song. If anyone saw them, they would think either they were happy in ages or had lost their mind.

Vishwas said, "You are not at all a lover boy. Where did you get this idea?"

"Before sitting down to write this, even I didn't have any idea that I could write so well, that too, a 'love story'."

"I have been in love every second day. Yaar, this story made me cry, too."

"*Arey, chal yaar, abhi mood na kharab kar* (Don't kill the vibe). There are some tandoori momos kept in the kitchen. Just bring them and make one more peg. I'm already swirling, dude. Just keep quiet and do as I'm saying," said Rachit.

"Okay, buddy."

"And yes, bring that mint chutney also that came along with momos, not the homemade one," Rachit shouted from outside.

"I am too high to differentiate between mint chutneys, Rachit!"

"Aah okay, bro," he continued to dance to loud music. Meanwhile, Vishwas came out with what Rachit had asked for – the Patiala peg this time – and they both continued dancing to Rachit's success.

Suddenly, a car stopped in the parking area, loaded with three to four men. They both could see a shadow from the second floor's balcony. They felt there was something fishy, to which Rachit volunteered to go and find out. They were getting down from the stairs with their momos plate in their hand, and Ms. Shaina was climbing up in the pretty *lakhnavi* embroidery suit. She was a journalist and disliked love stories to the core. That was evident from the look she gave Rachit while passing by. No one knew that the boy was in too much love with this pretty girl, and she was his inspiration behind the bestseller. Not even his only best friend knew that.

He gestured her to be silent, but her irritation for him was so much that she stepped forward, and as the guys were too drunk, they could not understand how to give her way. She ended up bumping into Rachit while he was mesmerised by her. The smell of her cologne was fresh even after coming back late from work. When she stepped back, the suit was no whiter. Instead, it was all green. The cologne now smelled like curd and mint. Shaina was too angry at them for spoiling her favourite suit. She was too frustrated and stormed off towards her house. Just then, there was a noise of a mirror breaking and glass shattering. All of them rushed to where the sound came. It was the same car that was parked a few minutes ago.

For a while, even Shaina was quiet and was not bothered about the suit anymore. The drunk boys were back to sober as there was a girl in that car whose hands were tied at the back, and she was gagged. She could not move. Vishwas asked Rachit to either call the police or leave the place right away, as he did not want to get into any kind of trouble.

"Bro, I haven't yet lost my virginity."

Shaina asked him to keep his mouth shut and asked him to call the police. Being a journalist, she was bold. So, she stepped forward to rescue the girl. Vishwas called the police and stopped Shaina from becoming '*Mardani.*' She didn't listen and somehow managed to pull out the girl from the broken window. The girl escaped and was now in her lap. She looked terrorised, and Shaina patted her head to make her comfortable. She sundered her from the car and moved towards the boys.

Rachit shouted at her to approach faster, but the three guys came and stood in front of her. They started laughing like maniacs as if they would treat her like Draupadi in Hastinapur's court, and she would be undraped. But she showed all her guts and kept on moving while carrying that pretty little girl. Those men followed her, but somehow, she was used to such silly conspiracies by the grace of her work. She felt pity for that little girl. Rachit approached Shaina to give her a helping hand but couldn't stand upright due to extreme alcohol consumption. By then, Vishwas was in his senses a bit. He was about to step closer to her, but just then, one tall man came in her way and held her from her hair to throw her on the ground.

The man uttered, "Support Mr. Dutta. This is just the beginning, my lady."

Shaina understood that this case was not about the girl. This was a shitty pothole related to Mr. Dutta's case. Mr. Dutta was an army veteran. Shaina had written an article in her column that became a huge headline last week. That article made Mrs. Sinha a little more frenetic as it could lead his only son to jail.

Hearing about this, Shaina shouted at Vishwas and Rachit to take the girl and call the police. Till then, she would move mountains to keep these nuts engaged somehow. Vishwas threw some chutney into Rachit's eyes to make him sober. It was the need of the hour. The thing worked. Rachit and Vishwas danced like apes as they knew no art of karate. The least they could do was to tickle them and run. They kept those two busy for a while and somehow managed to bring the little girl into their house. Meanwhile, the siren of a police car was also approaching them. The boys left the little girl in their apartment and locked the door. They climbed down the stairs and saw Shaina handing over those fools to the police.

Rachit was a little drenched in the joy of having the first conversation of his love story like this, a little different, just like Bollywood movies. Shaina handed her clutch to Rachit and ran towards the little girl. Suddenly, there was a huge blast, and everything went silent. Silent like the desert. Silent like a graveyard. Everyone was stunned by what had just happened. Shaina was lying down with an estranged leg. She could not say anything. She just looked into Rachit's eyes for the first and the last time. Rachit cried over and over, but he could not even say goodbye to his love. He opened his clutch to contact her family. The only thing he found was a little bottle of her cologne. He could not even say a word after that. On the night of the success of his first book, where he was lucky to see his lover every day, and now she was lying in his lap, dead.

The same day, 13th January 2020, he came up with his second bestselling novel, "Let me say I Love You." He celebrated that day with small kids in an orphanage as it was Shaina's only purpose of living. He put his hands in his pocket and took out a miniature bottle of her cologne which was the only thing left with him.

Seven

MELTED

"I'll fall, Didi. No, no, it's very difficult."

"You wanted to learn this, Ketki. Now, why are you saying no?"

"Come here. I'll sit behind you. *Ekdum satke.*"

"Hahaha," came a voice from somewhere. They both ignored it at first.

Then again came the same voice, "Your Didi, she herself is very feeble. How will she teach you? Come to me. Leave her," he said, followed by a popping sound from his mouth.

"Stretch your height a bit. Your feet won't reach the ground," someone out of them said anonymously.

There were many bystanders, but none interfered.

"Let's go, Didi," said Ketki.

"Keep your hands on the handles," uttered Lata.

"See her. Hahaha, there is no brake for them. Their feet are the brakes," chuckled another guy.

"Go home and cook food. The place where you belong."

Lata felt enervated in holding her irritation just then one of those men gestured horrendously by zipping up and down, which let Lata's anger know no bounds and she adorned his cheek with an exquisite slap.

"*Kamini* (voluptuous), I'll see you. You slut."

I know her whereabouts. Where she goes and what she does," he said in chorus.

She asked Ketki to shift to the back, and Lata drove to her place.

****

She opened the braid.

"Damn it. This scrunchy isn't coming out. Ugh."

She put all the effort she could to detach the scrunchy and threw it in the air.

"It was for me," she cried. "I was supposed to be there in her place. The trap was for me."

She broke out in grief as she walked towards the mirror. She loosened the salwar she was wearing. She stepped out of it as the salwar pooled on the floor. She then removed the shirt. She even removed her bra to see what was stopping her from being less smart or less germane for society.

Ketki was in the hospital for her second surgery, but it was supposed to be me, not her. Tears rolled down her cheek.

"Lata, this could have been you. Then your whole life would have been ruined. Nothing matters to these *sadak-chaap lafandars*. They are morons and see every woman as a toy. You also live alone, even though your parents are in the same city."

"Appa, please, I don't want to hear anything," she cried from her room.

"See. This girl is still not listening even after such a tragedy. Who would have married her if that had happened to her?"

"You calm down. She is already upset. We have to support her," said her *Aai* (mother).

"You are always supporting her in her wrong deeds. You are responsible for what has happened. First, supporting her becoming an independent woman, then living alone because she wants to be independent. People are already talking about us in the town. This is a small town, Mahe, and your daughter is too discreet for social norms."

****

"Didi, aapne na maza chakha diya un badmasho ko (What a lesson you have taught those monsters)."

"Ketki, don't talk about that crap. I am already very irritated about what has happened."

"Didi, I won't learn to drive a scooter now. I am very short for a scooter," said Ketki.

"Why, just because those morons said so? I am teaching you; how could you not learn?"

That evening, Lata decided to cook after months, just to cheer herself up. On the menu, there was Rajma that she had recently learned from her Punjabi colleague. She was an absolutely amazing cook, but her job didn't allow her much to be in the kitchen. Out of nowhere, until Rajma was being cooked, she decided to bake a chocolate caramel cake to soothe her mind. Her hands were all covered with flour and chocolate.

Just then, the bell rang.

"Ketki, can you go see who is at the door?"

"Oho, Didi. Sometimes you ask me to do a lot of work. Coming!" she cried from inside.

The doorbell rang three times in a row.

"Who is dying? Lord!" With gritted teeth, she stepped forward.

"Didi, I am in the washroom," said Ketki.

Lata washed her hands and moved towards the door to open it. She was about to touch the handle, but at the same moment, Ketki reached for the same and opened it.

"AAAAAA…AAAAAAAAA...."

Ketki was shocked. She could not move for a while. The boy ran with lightning speed after throwing the bottle of acid on the floor.

Ketki was writhing in pain. Lata picked up her phone and called the ambulance. Seeing her in pain, she could not wait any longer. She dragged Ketki towards her car and took her to the nearest hospital.

****

"Always remember, a girl should always be independent. Just the way you learned English on your own, one day you will complete your studies and will get a good job. That day isn't far when you'll buy your own scooter."

"I know you love me, but that doesn't mean you have to work for me all the time. I will not let that happen. Accha Didi, I'll go to meet Appa this weekend, the doctor said he needs to change the medicines so, I have saved some money, I will go and buy medicines for Appa."

"Sure, you may go, I have night shifts this weekend, so I'll not be there."

Just then, her phone rang.

"Yes, doctor. How's Ketki?"

"She is not fine. She is still unconscious, but her second surgery was successful. She will be in the ward, but no one is allowed to come too close to her, as there is a high risk of infection."

Lata dressed up shabbily, started her car, and reached the hospital in haste. She was standing near a big window and was aghast to see Ketki's condition from afar. Her body was now a living coffin, and under her eyes were shadows like charcoal clouds. The gaze was left in proper shape, rest all was dismantled on the degree of heat required for gold to acquire a new shape. The shell of her face had dropped like falling autumn leaves.

I can't go near her. I feel like I am responsible for this. I wouldn't have done that if..., she cried limitlessly.

Doctor Kritika, Lata's friend and a qualified doctor, came to her support. She said that it was not her fault. Ketki murmured just one thing, even in dizziness, "I'll definitely do it. I'll drive it."

You know, men love beautiful women. But when it's beauty and brains, they don't know how to handle it because we have no role models to emulate. Even our parents call such women 'too forward' when it's actually the men who are backward. Women are racing ahead, having kids and careers, leaving men holding their dicks in their hands. You know, at one time, girls were sent to finishing schools to increase their market value. Well, guess what? It's time for the men's finishing school. So, you let them taste the defeat.

****

Eight

DIVORCING MISOGYNY

"Your Dadaji (grandfather) is coming to Delhi after three days. He says he found a *rishta* for you. Meet the boy, at least. He is from our village, residing in Gurgaon for work. Earning a handsome salary. His wife left him with a 4-year-old kid due to cancer. He used to love his wife a lot. He doesn't have any problem in marrying a 'die-vorcee'."

This is what people here think. A divorcee is a die-vorcee for them, after which, a girl is a living dead. If not, then have variants of tags – *Kalmuhi* and all. And whatever she does is followed by a plethora of taunts in her platter.

****

It was dawn.

Strips of the barricade tape with "Do Not Cross" printed on them decorated the crime scene. Police sirens were hurling. It was the darkest night of my life. I had everything albeit having everything on barter – barter of my dreams, freedom, living, and what-not.

38

"Why did you do that? You strangled your mother. There is no bigger vamp than you I have ever seen," said the lady constable said. I wrapped my arms around my knees and cried hard.

"Your mother should have strangled a daughter like you in her womb."

She pushed me as hard as she could, and I woke up from the devilish dream, heaving for breath. I had just dreamt of killing my mother. My mother ran and asked what had happened.

"You don't let us sleep at ease even at night," another dose of taunt came. I hid myself under the blanket where not even an inch of light could enter.

Another morning, my mother reminded me that this time, whatever her Dada would speak, I was not supposed to insult him or even cross-question him about the man coming to see me.

My parents, with all enthusiasm, will once more play the game of fate. My fate was now a football that had to enter the right court, where the spectators could cheer, "Goal!"

I was quiet, with no words, as if to call my mother foundation less. Then again, I'd be called a big-mouthed girl with no sense of respect for elders. I was tired now; my mother's behaviour didn't even surprise me anymore. One day, she seemed to understand what I was going through, and the next, she would be my only foe who wanted to get rid of me.

My only problem now was that I had surrendered my life to the circumstances at the wrong point in time, enough to spoil my entire life after that. In regard to societal norms, I was often divulged as a tough child, as if every other child in my family was Shravan Kumar. I didn't give a damn about it. I was lonely, seeking the shoulder out of my family. The more I opened up with my secrets, the more I was trapped inside the walls.

It felt like they wanted to destroy my confidence, in which they succeeded, and I was in a trap of toxic relations just to support me for the time being. Gosh. Another setback. When the silent breakup happened, I was left with nothing. I wouldn't be marrying the person I loved. That boy was neither playing nor destroying me, just that he was becoming a 'raja beta' of his family, unlike me.

****

My father, a staunch believer that looks don't matter, had drooled when he saw the first *rishta* of an only child living in Dwarka. Two BHK, owned property, and a job met his meagre needs to get me off with him. He married me off just after one meeting at Bikaner Sweets at CP. I was sent out with him, where hardly anything made me click with him. I never had any wrong opinions for that guy in my mind. Neither did I have a long list of dos and don'ts or ifs and buts regarding a guy, except one thing. I was a passionate woman doing well in my career. I wanted a man to support me with my job who didn't judge me or my cooking or thought that cooking three meals a day was my duty. I had had a breakup just three days ago and was only twenty-six when I got married to Kamal. My life partner had been decided for me without my consent.

My dad had always wanted a girl who excelled in life in every segment, as if I were a trophy which he wanted to keep in a showcase to flaunt. On the contrary, I didn't excel in studies when I flunked in the second year of my English Honours. What my mind was weaving, then, was to find a job. Most of the students didn't know where they wanted to head, and I was one of them. I got a job at Air Canada. Within six months of joining, I got the opportunity to travel to Canada alone. I never knew neither the first time nor the fifteenth would be appreciated by my parents.

When I was twenty-six and married, my in-laws always called my parents to complain about me.

"She cooks as per her convenience. She doesn't have time to pamper Kamal. She doesn't ask much about anything from Kamal."

Blah... blah... blah... When I told my mother Kamal didn't even care to ask to join them before going for an evening walk with his mother every day, my mother said it was not a big deal.

"Your mother-in-law has a big list of dissatisfactions; you better take care of it." she would say.

I could barely live with such a relationship for nine months and came back when my mother-in-law raised her hand on me for putting a red handkerchief in the washing machine along with other clothes. God. Even my dad never had laid a finger on me. Kamal was standing like a mute spectator when I looked at him with little expectation of supporting me. Instead, he said that I had spoiled his mother's expensive white suit.

"Why wouldn't she be angry? Earning money is so hard."

"Oh, yes! I don't know how it is earned," I wanted to scream. I packed my bags and did not tell anyone before leaving for work the next day, and I went straight to my mother's house. Within three days, I found that the house was not mine anymore. Anyone who called during those days somehow dragged the conversation to whether I was pregnant yet or not.

Oh, God! I didn't get married to just be a Mommy and have a Valentine's baby. Whatever. Now my mother's sad tone gave people a chance to poke their noses in my life. From three days to a year, everything had happened. Most of all, I was dead internally. I started having anxiety whenever I went near my dad or talked about what was next. In awakening dreams, I saw ways to kill myself, being cursed by a lady constable for killing my own mother. I wish I could have killed this misogyny and patriarchy instead of having these vile dreams. My mother's foundation-less behaviour was also proof of loving me and pushing me into the same thing because she was answerable to the chronology.

****

The man coming to meet me this time was Dheer, and his son's name was Parth. During the meeting, he told me, "I like you, but my sole motive of marrying you will be Parth, as I can't move on from Shreya. Loving anyone else wouldn't do justice to her."

In my mind, I recalled the tagline of LIC, "*Zindagi ke saath bhi, zindagi ke baad bhi.*" I was so amazed to see a guy like him, yet I knew it would be another trauma for me when my dad said they had all liked him without looking at me, as if my opinion didn't matter. I felt like 'die-vorcing' my dad then and there. I closed my eyes and didn't let my tears flow out of the corner of my eyes. What they talked about after that faded, as if I was dreaming of a cupid carrying me. I felt so light. I could not hear what they were talking about anymore.

Darkness, slow and deep, calm, still, immobile, unbreathing, sweet sleep. No pain, no joy, no sight, no sound, no taste. I felt like I was floating far away. I didn't want to wake up. I would rather stay in this cotton-wool-like world. Its sweet, sleepy melody seemed to carry me up through the ceiling, the bannisters, the rooms up above, through the entire weight of the building, its steeple. I rose like a cloud wisp at one go and left the meeting. I didn't care about this family anymore. Before the family members reached home. I took my documents, a few clothes, and was ready. I was a thirty-year-old woman who was finally taking charge of her life, and I was not going to look back.

I didn't know where I would go, or what I would eat. I might even die the next moment, yet it was still better than dying every day anymore. And to my happiness, my parents never tried to be in touch with me, ever again.

Nine

AN UNEXPECTED MOTHER

"Stop, stop. Ha-ha, stop, Janya. No more water for me. I don't like being wet."

Janya flapped her hands to and fro and laughed aloud.

"Wash the soap foam, take this towel, and come out."

Janya gave her hand to Maithili, making variant noises, and Maithili helped her come out of the bathtub. Janya seemed heavy nowadays. She was grown up now. Five years went by with lightning speed.

****

Five years ago.

"Abhay, please listen to me."

"No, Maithili. This is ridiculous. You are twenty-eight. We are *rokafied* (engaged), and this is what I am hearing from you. I am sorry I can't tell my parents this. I have to break the relationship."

"No, no, Abhay. I love you." She broke down. "You can't do this to me. We have been together for four years. You love me, too. I know you do."

Abhay didn't listen to her. He jerked her hands away and boarded the metro. Maithili stood there for a good fifteen minutes, whining without caring what people would think of her. The love of her life had just left her. She gathered herself after crying her heart out. The man she thought would be there all her life just left her for something for which she wasn't even responsible.

****

She still remembered holding Janya in her arms for the first time, the first kiss she placed on her head. She took a bath and then helped Janya dress up.

"You are just like her mom. You are so sweet, Maithili. It is high time you get married. Your biological clock is ticking. You should get married and have your own kid. Why are you sacrificing your life for this mental?" uttered Darshana aunty. The fat, heavy-hipped *Chachi* (aunt) of mine, whenever I see her, I feel she is carrying Wagon-R car's backside or as if she has a walking sofa at her back.

"*Ji* (okay), *Chachi*. I'll see if I can find a guy."

"The one you found couldn't resist your parents. Poor you."

"Why *Chachi*? My parents are my responsibility, same as Janya."

We make choices sometimes through what life throws at us. Happy or not, they become our inevitable truth.

Just then, Maithili's phone rang. The sound broke her circle of thoughts. It was Aman, her colleague.

"Hello. Yes, Aman. I have sent the desired details. Just cross-check them before you forward it to the boss."

"That's not what I called you for."

"Then?" she sounded amazed.

"It's because you aren't coming for the evening get-together. Why did you say no? It is not even late. You know you always miss such get-togethers. All the limelight will fall on Srishti. You have worked hard on the project. You must be there."

"Leave it, Aman. I can't come. I have responsibilities."

"I understand, but...."

She interrupted him and said, "See you in an hour for the presentation."

"Okay, then," he said, and she disconnected.

For these reasons, I didn't get too close to the folks at work. They'd all make plans to go out to eat after work. They referred to it as decompression. To enjoy oneself. I had to return home so that my parents would not be concerned about anything bad happening to me. But it was more to appease the many aunties in the family who were outraged that my parents were "letting me work" instead of marrying me, she thought.

"*Arey chali jati na. Office main thodi time milta hoga extra baat karne ka. Jayegi nahi to koi ladka kaise milega? Boyfriend-shoyfriend to aise hi milte hai. Tu hi dhoond. Kab tak is pagal ki dekhbhaal karegi? Tere maa-baap ko toh apne se fursat nahi hai* (You should have gone. You definitely don't get leisure time during work hours. How will you ever get a guy if you don't go out? That is how you make a boyfriend. How long will you take care of this mad child? You will have to find a guy for yourself, as your parents can't get over themselves)," taunted Sudha *tai* (aunt), ridiculing Maithili.

That very moment she felt like replying, "*Tai*, you aren't old enough to make one," but she chose to keep quiet.

****

"Beta, we made a mistake. Your father and I were seriously guilty of taking away the charming life from you and putting the load of her on your shoulders. Think about your life now. Janya is our responsibility. We will take care of her."

"Maa, I know what my life is. It's Papa, you and Janya. I realised it when Abhay left me, and Janya came to me. Janya is more of my daughter than my sister. You had her when I was twenty-eight, but now at thirty-three, I feel I am a mother of a five-year-old. I don't need a man. Janya needs particular care as she is fragile."

She said that, and suddenly there was a sound of panic. The upheavals could be heard from Maithili's room, as if a catastrophe had happened.

Maithili ran and found Janya out of control. She had blood flowing out of her ears. It generally happened when Janya got hyper. She quickly texted Aman to start the meeting, and she would join in soon.

Abhay had left her on the note that I could not give place to anyone. She wished life could have been like a fictional story with a happily ever after: her parents would have been accepted by society, by her fiancé, but none of that happened.

Ten

A GIFT OF LIFE

Deaths are sad, incredibly sad, but they are also meant to bridge the gap which has been there for a decade.

Mine was a family who loved to eat together, sing old songs together, drink together, even sleep together. The best part was when the summer holidays rolled in. We got an opportunity to get creative, or if I must say, it was me who enfolded her creative side by doing all of my eight cousins' work.

Yes, our crazy family of almost twenty-three people lived together. My grandfather had been married twice and hence, had seven kids. Years passed, everyone got married and had their own families. Still, we lived like one. The question of having separate gas burners was never an idea for us. But there were families splitting every month in our neighbourhood. My grandparents had kept all of us together.

It was June 2008. I was in the ninth grade and had just created a functional model of a windmill. I was very excited. I ran to my youngest uncle's room, who wasn't there. I ran to Bittu *Chacha's (uncle's)* room, but he wasn't there either. I thought they both were out somewhere, so I ran to Kamlesh Chacha's room, but didn't find him, too. I got a little irritated as my excitement knew no bounds. I wanted to show my project to my beloved uncles as soon as possible. I ran to the fields and saw that all three of them were loudly talking as if there would be bloodshed in the next fifteen minutes. I wanted to go nearer, but before I could take a step, there was a gunshot.

Everything was silent. I was almost deaf. More than that, I was numb. I gathered myself and ran towards my grandfather. He was lying on the ground. He had been shot in the head and had died on the spot. It was Makhija who was after our family to give up our ancestors' piece of land, which my grandparents weren't willing to. All my uncles were ready to accept the proposal, as they thought it wasn't good to mess with this political triumph who not only had great connections but was also the most powerful in our village.

I had lost my parents just after a year of birth. I could only see their photos hanging in our house. It was my uncles and my grandparents who never let me feel like an orphan. Dadaji's death was a big stroke for our family. No one was talking to one another, and even my grandmother was blaming my uncles for my grandfather's death. I was sharing my grandmother's room.

Today was my grandmother's 70th birthday, and I was turning twenty-five. Growing up, I have gotten the features of my mother. My mother was indeed the most beautiful angel on this earth, but I couldn't compete with her, but that day, my grandmother was behaving weirdly. Rolling a rosary, a little faster, as if she were having an anxiety attack. Silver water pearls were rolling from the side of her neck.

Was it a heart attack? No, that couldn't happen. First, I had lost my parents, then my grandfather, and now on grandma's birthday, Dadi was having a heart attack. God couldn't be so cruel.

My Dadi called me before I could raise my voice to summon anyone. I could feel the somnolent air, but she said, "You are here with us because your grandfather isn't with us."

I was amazed. What was she saying?

She loved grandfather a lot. She used to worship him every day.

"It wasn't Makhija who shot your Dada. It was me who took advantage of the fight between Makhija and your Dada. You were almost sold to Makhija by your Dada, even after your uncles were vexed about it. Bittu was furious about his decision, but your Dadaji never listened to anyone. His love was just a whimsical presentation. He always considered you a bad omen who took his children away from him. I couldn't see him doing this to you, so I shot him that day."

I almost lost everything that day, even after knowing that my Dadi had lost more than me. I was a gift to myself because of her.

Eleven

A FRIENDSHIP: TO MAKE OR MAR?

"*Aye*, what exactly is this?"

"This is a mountain, a large river, trees, and a small home, to be exact," Aditya responded by pointing to a scribbled wooden desk.

"Oh, no! Teacher...teacher...."

'Yes, Akshara. What happened?"

"Aditya is ruining the school's property."

With a frown, Ms. D'Costa turned to Aditya.

"What is this, Aditya? It's horrifying to see you doing this. Where is your diary? Give it to me."

In his diary, she wrote a not-so-mollycoddling article. Of which he showed no regret and kept it in his pocket.

****

Later that day, he was pondering near the water cooler when Akshara appeared and said, "Solly," mimicking and not meaning it at all.

"Akshara, please."

She seemed to be a bully. He left the place with a nonchalant shrug at her.

Aditya used to be 'the most wanted *munda*' of the school, and that irritated Akshara a lot. He was rich and an over-privileged child. Akshara was a daughter of an Army man and bound to strict discipline even at home. For her, Aditya was nothing apart from a rich MLA's son.

The next day in the Physics lecture, Akshara was seated behind Aditya, and during the 15 minutes test, she saw Aditya sketching instead of answering the MCQs.

"Teacher…teacher…."

"What happened? Is there any problem with you, Akshara?"

"Look at Aditya. What is he doing?"

The teacher was annoyed.

"Both of you leave my class. Leave these Tom and Jerry moments out of my class."

The whole class uncontrollably chortled. The teacher frowned, and all the heads were back to the sheets.

****

"Why don't you leave me alone?" sighed Aditya.

"What did I do? You don't remember what you were doing?"

"That is none of your business."

The argument turned into a heated fight until Aditya gripped Akshara's hand, and the teacher came out. They both were suspended for a fortnight.

Akshara was angry about what just happened, yet she had an urge to go back to Aditya, not to apologise, but to ask about the scars he had on the back of his arm. The time was strenuous. She wanted to go back and ask him what that was.

Had he tried to hurt himself? Was he hard on himself regarding something? She could not stop herself and reached his house, a lavish mansion at Anand-Niketan. She met him and apologised for what she had done. His parents also forgave her and asked them to bond like friends. It was difficult for him, yet he didn't utter anything and accepted the friendship.

"Our life is a retrospect of the good and the bad times!"

****

Akshara was sitting at her daughter's school, demanding the principal about the scars she saw on her daughter's forearms and the change in her behaviour.

The principal tried to ask Siya about how it happened., but she chose to keep quiet.

The principal understood Akshara's pain and assured her that it would be sorted in not more than two to three days.

"Why do you think every incident is related to that one? Siya is a child, and she might have had a fight with someone and is scared to share, thinking she will also be scrutinised."

"Maa, please, times are tough. These days, sending daughters to school or anywhere alone is not an easy task for any mother, or even for a boy, it never was."

"Oh, please, Akshara. Not again. You have already lost everything due to that boy. I wish you would have never befriended him," she added. "Oh yes, I knew. I always know when he's here and what all you're up to. But you must understand that you're older now. Just like childhood ended, school ended, college ended, your childish best-friendship with that boy also has to come to an end."

"Do you think Aditya was wrong, Maa?"

"Yes. Just because his parents had a tough time together, he cooked up stories. I still think he used to hurt himself to punish himself."

"Oh, Mumma. Not again. He wasn't. He just could not talk about the nuisance that was happening to him. He could not talk to his parents about that vile man who exploited Aditya being at his house."

"Shut up, Akshara. I don't think something that much has happened to Siya. You are hyping it too much."

"Haan, Maa. I can see a change in my daughter's voice and her way of seeing others. She is always busy sketching. She doesn't do much."

"Arey, kids change a lot while growing up. Look at yourself."

She didn't listen! She knew that it was the same thing. After a struggle of five weeks, she came to know about the bus driver exploiting her daughter for fancy things. He confessed that once he asked her to kiss him. With god's grace, it wasn't a rape, yet the weekly events between her daughter and driver tattered the soul of her daughter.

She once again had to work the same way with her daughter the way she had worked with a friend to forget the incidents of boyhood. She cried a lot that night. No matter a boy or a girl, it could happen to anyone, at any age. Her daughter was just six. She, at the right time, caught that, else god knows what would have happened.

****

"Again, these scars. Aditya, it seems someone held you from your neck."

He cried his heart out for the first time on Akshara's shoulders. With moist eyes, he confessed, "I can't tell this to everyone. My parents keep on fighting for that person to stay or to leave the house. It's like a war. I don't know why they are putting up together. I am tired of these everyday battles, and moreover, he knows my father needs him for his party promotions. According to him, he is *'kaam ka banda'* (a useful resource). It is him who takes advantage and exploits me for his pleasure. I am tired of it, Akshara. I'll die. Help me!"

She assumed him hanging and shunned, so she assured him she would help.

That day, Aditya saw a sort of spark in Akshara's eyes as if she was going to do something to save her friend. She not only helped her friend to unravel the reality by filming his uncle's evil deeds, but also helped him to recover from the trauma by diverting him towards other things.

This made them best friends, which to some extent, Akshara's parents didn't like, and to date, they curse Aditya for Akshara's divorce, too.

Twelve

SABOTAGE

It was never my intention. There were many ways of giving that judgment, but the most stringent way was to bang the hammer that day rather than postpone it for the next session. The scar of his life imprisonment on his family was indeed a deepened one which might never fade away.

Since that afternoon of March, Mohan's words haunted Richa. Indeed, it was her job, and such threats were sophomoric. Still, they had weight, and the night always brought back memories for Richa. Shadows seemed to come alive and haunt her, repeatedly reminding her that the ordeal was far from over. The lovemaking, the chitchatting, the pious promises of living together for the next seven reincarnations, and the last words, "I promise this will cost you your life," were buzzing in her ears.

She was spreading semi-solid butter on bread with a plastic spoon. As she came out of her pondering, she found the bread in pieces due to the force she was putting on it. One piece of it fell flat on the corner of the shelf.

Mohan was granted bail six months ago, and no one knew where he was. Someone at work told her that he died in an accident, but she knew only the good die young. She was six months pregnant with Abhi's (her husband's) child, and it had been almost 5 years since the judgement she had given against Mohan, her then fiancé. Never in her dreams had she thought that Mohan could kill someone. That, too, just because he could not control his anger. Two long years she had dated him, but she wasn't gullible. As a High-court judge, she had a strong personality with an indomitable will. Still, she oversaw his personality as a gentleman. He was a gazetted officer with a split personality. A personality where he couldn't see the good in someone at a lower rank. To him, people were inferior if they weren't educated or were working on meagre profiles. She heard the landline ring. It was Abhi. He sounded anxious, as if he had seen a ghost.

He asked how she was, and she replied, "First-class. The baby is craving for a bucket of a sundae, so I was thinking of grabbing one right now."

"No need to step out. I'll call the Niceland grocery store, and the owner will send his boy. I will be there in an hour. Okay?"

After disconnecting, she turned, and something banged so hard on her face that in a few seconds, everything was out of order. She could not hear anything.

It was Mohan, who had snuck into her kitchen in the disguise of her cleaner. He didn't let her shout or create any nuisance as he had a bottle of acid in his hands.

"Mohan, what's wrong with you? How could you have been this mean? I can't imagine you doing this in my deadliest dreams."

"Oh, wow. You promised to be on my side, and there is a child of a *munshi* (C.A) in your womb. You are his wife after giving me a living death. You could have saved me, bitch!"

"Ah!" She was groaning as if she had a headache.

She gathered a little strength and said, "I never knew you had personality issues. We were about to get hitched before that incident, and for me, my work and personal life are two different poles. I could not save my paranoid fiancé and then get married to him and ruin my life, too."

"Why not? Let me tell you what happens when you belittle someone's love."

He was opening the bottle of acid, and just then, she took the tiny broken piece of a plastic spoon and aimed for his eye. As he was startled, the acid spilled on his thighs, and a little bit spilled on Richa's hand, too. Just then, the doorbell rang. She knew it was Adi, the boy from the grocery store. As she could not get up and Adi heard the screams of a man, he rushed back to the shop. He fetched the owner with him, saying, "*Didi* (sister) is in trouble."

The owner called Abhi, who was already 15 minutes away from the house but was stuck in a traffic jam.

Richa rushed to another room and locked herself. Due to anxiety, she started to bleed.

That afternoon of March, and today, one thing was common, Richa was regretting her choice. Mohan tried to kill her the same way he had killed innocent Jaya. She had mistakenly dented his brand-new car and was saying sorry for the same. She had reasoned that she was getting late for her office and her boss would fire her if she arrived late. She did not know that she would never make it that day.

All the doors were locked, and Richa was inside her bedroom. She was scared to death after recalling the photos of Jaya's dead body she saw in the court. The grocery shop owner, police, and Adi were outside, but Mohan seemed to have nothing to lose and was still inside. He was trying to break the lock of her room in order to have a hold of her.

However, as he opened the door of her room, they managed to cut the main lock. The police officers held him. He was screaming for his failure more than his agony of an acid spill. This is what a feeling of sabotage could do to a man.

Richa was blessed to be saved just in time, though the terror of Mohan would always remain. Despite being a judge, she could not be spared from male-broken hysteria.

Thirteen

THE RED CARPET

Neeti, full of life, jerked at decisions but cared the least about what people said.

Folks had already made an assumption that a missing feminine influence in life was the reason for her boldness. "Poor motherless daughter."

Prakriti, her best friend, was no different to her. No wonder 'the duo' was so similar. No, Prakriti did have a mom, yet she didn't like the way she surrendered herself to these assumptions. Maybe that had made Prakriti bold.

"Prakriti, why do you always contradict your name?" uttered Sheila, her mother. "*Ye saara asar us bin maa ki beti ka hai* (this is the influence of your motherless friend)."

"Mummy, please, you know it well. I never like hearing this, neither in front of her, nor behind her back. So, stop saying that. Moreover, I never contradict my name. Prakriti means 'nature' and who knows well to take down things when they leave their roots. You know earthquakes, floods and all."

"Hey, *Bhagwan*, it's better to keep mum."

"As you wish and feel like. Anyway, I am going to meet Neeti. I am showing her Mohit's picture, else she will kill me."

"Haan, zaroor jao. Rishta abhi abhi hua hai. Tumhe samajh nahi aata na? (Sure, do go. You never understand that it's a new thing.)"

"She will not jinx it for sure."

Later that evening, the friend duo met.

"You told me everything is done as Mohit wanted. He must have included you in his decisions."

"No, *yaar.* You know our work timings clash."

"Prakriti, are you really extremely excited, or are you just overseeing it?"

"Neeti, you should be happy that I'm getting married."

"I certainly am. But I know my friend in a different way. This changed version is short-lived."

"Whatever. I got busier in preparations and work. Mohit always made time out of his busy schedule during our courtship. So, I can't meet you, Neeti, as he is meeting me after five days. I'll catch you tomorrow."

"But we planned that movie together. Next time, please."

"Okay."

Soon, the day of the marriage came.

Prakriti was the most nervous bride on the planet. That could be seen in the wedding album. With all that crying at '*Vidai*', things changed overnight for her, but there was hardly any change in Mohit's schedule. As a result, she was not even allowed to talk about it. Was she supposed to click a mute button?

Prakriti did not understand. So, she kept quiet all this while. There weren't even any calls between her and Neeti. So, she indulged in my favourite time pass. She read a lot and ordered books, free, audio, Kindle, the ones waiting on her wish list for so long.

Mohit had never raised his hand on Prakriti, had never taken or asked for dowry; he didn't even drink, not even occasionally. He could have been in an affair as he was so charming. But so was she.

There was a bang. Prakriti's mother had slapped her, and she was in tears. How couldn't she understand? Prakriti's alter ego murmured that her mother herself was a victim of misogyny, of patriarchy, of submissiveness, so she wouldn't understand. Her marriage herself was neither happy nor sad, and always lacked a pinch of emotion.

Her mother leaned forward and said, "I know you don't want to become that old couple celebrating the birth of your granddaughter without holding hands and him complimenting your beauty at fifty. So, I, as a mother, can't say anything. But for you, it will be a road full of shattered glass covered with dry leaves as divorce is a sin in our family, and in your case, there is not even ground to it."

Her mother left the room after saying this, and that night, neither of them could sleep.

Day after day, Sheila was turning more spiritual than ever before. Only her God knew what went behind her prayers. She started ignoring her daughter's calls. Prakriti was sure with each passing moment that she was not the same. Every call, her father said that her mother was either in the temple or reading some mythological book. She understood for sure that her mother would not help her with this. She kept on reading her favourite book on repeat, something she had never done before, as she used to read every book once and adore it in her library as an asset.

That evening, Prakriti's father called her many times, but she didn't answer. He kept calling to entail her daughter in her mother's search, as Sheila had been out since 5 a.m. and had not even taken her phone with her. The unanswered calls from Prakriti made her father even more worried. Just then, he saw Sheila getting off an auto. He straight went to her and was furious with her.

"Oh, wow. So, you were out to get a cut like this. What happened to your perfectly ordinary pigtail I always loved?"

She kept quiet as always, but for the first time, her body language was full of guilt, regret; not for herself, but for her daughter. She walked off with Prakriti and Neeti like a walk on a red carpet and ordered her husband to bring three cups of tea.

****

Sheila had called Neeti at 6:30 a.m. Neeti was frightened at first, but relieved at another moment. Neeti quickly inferred that she was sounding different today. Sheila asked to catch her up at 8. By then, Mohit would also leave for his meeting, and they had something urgent to do before they met Prakriti.

Around 10:20, they reached Prakriti's house, but she didn't answer the door. They tried again and confirmed she hadn't gone out, as her car was parked in its place. Just then, they heard something concrete hit the ground hard. Neeti estranged herself from Sheila and moved to the nearest window. What they found was not acceptable to their eyes.

They broke into her house. Sheila cried and just saved her precious daughter. They untied the thin crape piece of cloth around her neck, and they both cried to see the bold Prakriti taking such a drastic step. The marriage, she never thought of was such an ungainly affection and filled with days of quiet. Sheila realised even the strongest person needed an ally. She was happy she had saved her daughter just in time.

Fourteen

THE COMMITMENT

"Go, Papa. I'll wait for you here in the car. Bring mummy's reports while I reverse the car, and I'll be there in the parking lot."

She unlocked the car, and her father shut the door. But then she honked loudly and continuously. Her father turned towards the car and opened it. She said, "You forgot the mask. They won't let you in."

"Oh my god, how could I? Maybe it is a short drive here, so neither you nor I noticed that I don't have one. Do you have extra one in your car?"

"No, Papa. You sit here in the car. I'll go upstairs."

"No, no. Don't lock the car this way, Papa. Press this button when I'm back."

SDAR Laboratory was written at the entrance, too bold, and could be seen from far away. The entrance was tight, though. Moreover, it was almost 8:00 p.m., time to close the lab. She asked the guard for the way to the reception.

"Third floor, Madam."

She got into the lift and pressed the floor button. The doors opened; it didn't seem like the reception of the laboratory. The place felt like a shaft sort of dingy area, covered by a French glass window in front and normal glass on the other two sides. She stepped out of the elevator, and for once, felt like 'Bruce Almighty' might happen to her. She had a notion that she was in the right place.

Papa is waiting in the car. He told me to climb this building, she thought. She looked here and there and realised her crazy mistake.

"This building doesn't have a ground floor. The third floor is actually the fourth. Ugh, this is the terrace," she cursed herself for getting late.

She turned towards the lift, pressed the button, and while waiting for the doors to open, she heard someone sobbing, followed by a thundering bawling voice, and a thud on the door. The sobs turned into wails. Someone just left after thundering in anger, but a girl in her early twenties or late teens was still crying while wrapping her arms around her knees. She was wearing tights as if she was working out a minute ago.

The lift doors opened, and I got into it. So many thoughts in my mind.

Is it child abuse? Is she his daughter? His wife? His maid? Maids don't wear such expensive workout clothes. Why was he hitting her? Was he really hitting or just scolding?

The doors opened again, and there was the reception. The receptionist was a man in his mid-forties who resembled a Tamilian.

I told my mother's name, and the man at the reception was taking the printout.

He could tell me about the girl.

"*Bhaiya* (Brother), does anyone live upstairs?"

"Upstairs? No, Madam. But the second and first floor is occupied by a family."

"This lab?"

"This, too. The whole building belongs to one family."

"Madam, you look tensed. Is everything okay?"

"Yeah, um... yes. Everything is fine. Could you tell me one thing?"

"Yes, please."

"I saw a girl on the terrace. Mistakenly, I pressed the 3rd floor."

"She must be doing Zumba. She is the daughter of the owner of the building. The owner lives in the U.S., his daughter lives here. She is doing medical studies. The owner was back this morning."

She saw her clock. *Oops, papa is still waiting.* She rushed towards the car. The moment she came near the car, her papa grew restless and started scolding her.

"What was it? Were you making the reports by yourself?"

"I'll tell you, Papa," she manoeuvred towards the driving seat. In front of her eyes, something fell, and an ear-splitting thud was heard. She was stunned. She rushed back, her father behind her.

"What happened?"

She felt strange chaos in the entire building. The receptionist was calling the ambulance.

"What happened?"

No reply.

"I asked what happened?"

"The girl, the owner's daughter, just fell, Madam."

She rushed towards the site. The pool of blood was around her. She went closer. The girl's father was also there, shouting, "Idiot, girl. Why did you do it? Why?" He was howling. "I didn't scold you to do this," he cursed himself. His hands were full of blood.

"She will not survive," Piya talked to herself. She stood there, teary-eyed. She didn't understand. Was this the reason she was anxious when she saw her? Was she already feeling strange about this catastrophe to be occurring? Whatever. The ambulance came, and she had been shifted to it.

***

"Studying medicine doesn't mean you can promote the shit. I am a person who lives in a society, who doesn't accept my daughter to fall in love with someone alike."

"What alike? Why don't you say same-sex or same orientation? Is it hideous or foul invective or a curse? That's me, Dad," said Zora.

"First, you changed your name to Zora from Zohra. That I accepted, but this. Are you out of your mind? I shifted to the U.S. but never forgot the roots."

"Dad, that's not about forgetting roots. That's who I am. Haven't you known Ricky?"

"Oh, please. No, we all know he is gay. And in an elaborated manner, he is a trans."

"No, Dad."

"Just shut up. Forget about all this. Complete your studies. Stay away from Anahita. I'll talk to her father as well. And we will see a psychiatrist."

"I am not suffering from depression or mental imbalance," shouted Zora.

He slapped her and departed, terminating the conversation.

****

"Lagta hai kuch hua he. Kahi saab ko pata to ni laga. (Something has happened. Did Sir find out about his daughter?) Both girls. Hahaha," the receptionist was talking to the ward boy in a broken Hindi-Tamilian tone.

Piya gave them a cold glance and started following the ambulance in her car. Her father asked her why she was bothered. She didn't answer.

****

Zora was inside the OT.

"Excuse me, sir. I mistakenly heard the talk between you and your daughter," Piya said and narrated how she had reached the terrace. "You should have listened to what she wanted to say. You should not have quietened her."

"What do you know? I love my daughter but accepting her as a lesbian is such a shame. A girl must date a boy."

Piya was shocked to know that her tact was successful and sad at the same time.

"There is shame in accepting who we are? You aren't liberated if you talk like this."

"Liberalism doesn't mean having intimacy with the same sex."

"It's a personal choice."

****

She kept visiting Zora every day. Zora finally gained consciousness after a month. She introduced herself to Zora with a box of chocolates. They laughed, giggled, and became friends. She looked at her with love, and Piya uttered, "I'm already committed, but she is yours," she said, giving Anahita's hand to her.

Fifteen

THE BADNAAM GULLY

30th July 1999

LOC, Kashmir

"Chaand, I'm coming home, but nothing remains the same. Everything has changed. I have changed. Everything has a new meaning. I have seen the fatal deaths of my friends in these two months," Ranjit sobs. "Chaand how is everyone at home?"

"Major Saab, everything is the same as you left it here. Both the parents are waiting to solemnise the wedding, which you left in between to serve our country. I am a proud wife of Major Saab," she stopped after saying this, as if she wanted to say something more but found it wasn't an appropriate time.

Ranjit knew her well. *"Keh tu, ki kehna hai* (Say what you want to say)."

"Tussi ghare aao, bahot kuch kehna hai. Te ikk khushkhabri vi hai (You come home. I have a lot to say, and have good news, too)."

"Tell me now. Maybe I'll have a reason to come home soon."

"You are going to be a daddy."

Ranjit was elated to hear this, yet the bloodshed of a few days back was moving to and fro in front of his eyes.

"Chaand, does anyone else know about this?"

"Do you want me to be dead by the time you'll be back? We aren't married yet, Major Saab. *Je, papaji nu pata laggeya na, te muh tod dena hai mera* (If my dad gets to know this, he will break my face)."

Suddenly, Ranjit started groaning in pain.

"What happened?"

"Nothing, I too have a souvenir of this deadly war. I had four bullets in my waist. It's been treated now. I'll be home soon, Chaand. Promise me you'll convince our parents to have a simple marriage. I don't find this time appropriate to have a grand one."

"Hmm," she agreed.

****

8th August 1999

"May you forever shine like this. God has given you the chance to adorn the vermillion on your forehead."

It was a great battle. Many lost their beloved. Her mother put a red dupatta over her head and kissed it gently. All the family members decided to celebrate her Mehendi night when she would put henna on her hands. The following day, Ranjit and Chandni would get married in the village's Gurudwara. A Thar came, and two people jumped down with bad news.

"We received our brother's belongings today in a trunk wrapped in tricolour," said Ranjit's brother.

They narrated that on 4th August, he got a cardiac arrest due to the treatment he was going through to remove the bullets. He was recovering, but something unexpected happened. He would be counted as a martyr of the Kargil war.

Chandni fainted and fell to the ground. After gaining consciousness, she cried and cried, then stood up and requested to come with them and meet the grief-stricken in-laws. She waited till the cremation ended. She then talked to her in-laws and told them about the fruit of their family that she bore with her.

She was expecting a smile. That, for a while, they would forget the trauma and embrace their grandchild along with her mother. Ranjit's mother came forward and slapped her.

"Are you out of your mind? The last time when he came was just for two days until he received an unexpected call of duty."

"Mummyji, please listen to me."

"You are a vile lady. You always gave Ranjit an assurance that you'll love him as well as accept his first love for this country as your own, yet you did this."

His mother couldn't speak further, as if she was falling short of cursing words. Then Ranjit's brother came forward and dragged her outside the house and asked her to get back in the jeep.

"Just because I wished you were my sister-in-law, I am leaving you back at your place, else I would have killed you right here."

She cried, but no one heard her plight. Going back, her own family disowned her and banished her from the village. She had the thought of killing herself and the tiny soul inside her, but it was the last memory of Ranjit she had. She then boarded a train without knowing where she was heading.

****

"Mummy, I am all right. Please, let me play. It's a tiny wound. I am a brave girl."

"I know Shama is a brave girl. But, baby, listen. Don't go to that street. Tell your friends to play hide 'n' seek nearby. That lane is not safe."

"Mumma, that aunty is charming. The red dress she is wearing is captivating. You also ask papa to buy you that saree."

"Umm, okay." The lady ended the conversation so as not to take it any further.

****

The ringing telephone pierced through the silence. Chandni ran to answer it.

"Hello! There is a customer, ma'am."

"For how many days?"

"Three nights and four days."

"When will he check in?"

"Monday."

"Okay, the room will be prepared," she said and then started to clean the room and change the toiletries.

****

The sound of the train pulling away from the platform was the only thing heard in the background. As the signboard said, this was Bareilly. The platform was deserted. There are a few rickshaw drivers waiting for passengers. There were no coolies at this time of the night. Despite the fact that Chandni did not have any luggage, she was terrified on a deserted platform.

"Aee... Chh... Chh… Shhh…" It was a beckoning from a gully boy. She noticed.

She began to run. She couldn't even take a rickshaw because she didn't have a destination. She disembarked from the train that had come to an end. She came to a halt. She had a thirsty feeling.

"Could you please tell me this address, dear?"

"I'm sorry. I'm new to town, Uncle," she started to say, then

72

paused. She reasoned that being with him would help her stay safe. "But I believe I can assist you with the address."

She noticed the hoardings; it was the same place the uncle was looking for. And she began looking for the figures. She might drive him to his residence. Once there, she knocked three times. A woman in her forties arrived.

"What were you doing? Did you miss your way home once again?"

"This kind lady assisted me. I was on the other side of the road, close to the track," the man said. "Do you have any plans for the evening? This area is dangerous. You are welcome to come in and make yourself at home."

With the passage of time, the elderly couple evolved into a new family.

All of the wounds had grown old by this point. They seemed to be less painful now. The elderly couple seemed to be in love like two children, but old age came with a slew of health issues. She nursed them, and the uncle appeared to be very proud of Chandni, saying that her son would become a soldier like her father. She had to send her only son to boarding school because she felt that living in this place, where everyone was always asking about his father, would make it difficult for her to survive. She seemed to be less taken aback by incivility directed at her.

****

"Are you paying attention?"

"Shama was in the neighbourhood today."

"What do you desire?"

"Our daughter has made a new friend with the scarlet lady."

"Hold on. First and foremost, watch what you say. We have no evidence to support such a claim.

That is precisely why I could not, to date, kick her out. She has been open for men every other day or week since uncle aunty died."

"This is now out of control. Why hasn't she married yet? She used to have a swollen stomach. No one in the area knows where her son is. There will be no husband."

"Do something for the sake of our daughter."

****

Knock, knock! Knock, knock! Knock, knock!

"Yes, welcome. Do you have identification, proof?"

"Yes, absolutely."

"Okay, I've arrived for my test. I'll be here for four days."

"Sure thing."

"See, I'm telling you. This lady is up to no good. Look, another visitor," That one lady pulled the rest of the citizens into cursing innocent Chandni.

She pounded on the door, ignoring the illegitimate howling.

"Didi, why don't we make room for ladies and families? "

"That's a good point. There are two explanations for this. One, we aren't yet liberal enough in the small town for me to get solo ladies. I sometimes get a squad of a few ladies. That's rare, though. I would tell, for families. I really don't have a heart. These men come and stay at a fair price, and the money is sufficient for my survival," she honestly answered.

"This lady clearly lacks the courage to confront us. She has turned our lane into a *Badnaam Gully*. Huh.

This is sufficient. I'm going to file a complaint against her and try to get rid of this germ. She is not a good influence for our children."

****

"Here's some breaking news. After 8 hours of firing, a CBI officer, Digvijay Singh Bhuttar, seems now to win the long battle against three terrorists."

"Mummy, come here, sit beside me. See this photo on T.V. Doesn't he look like our brother?"

"Haan, Haan, puttar (Yes, Yes, kiddo). It's as if Ranjit is in front of me. Who is he?"

"The name on the screen says Digvijay Singh Bhuttar."

"What? Bhuttar? That is our name."

"I was thinking the same. He is a CBI officer who is being reported by a well-known news channel. They are tallying his many accomplishments. The same face cut. Is he...?"

"Arey, naah, naah. (No, No.) That is not possible."

Just then, the extended media coverage attracted the attention of the whole family. The headlines flashed. Digvijay's father had also been a Kargil war martyr. Indeed, brave blood. The jaws dropped!

The mother started howling at her doing. Still, some deeds were irreplaceable. Time could be a big healer.

"If our grandson is such a successful man, maybe our daughter is, too. Find her. It's time to bring her home with my grandson."

"Hanji (Alright)."

****

Three days later, in the evening, there was a gathering of people. All fingers pointed towards the door of Chandni's house. The house the elder couple gave her resulted from no heir of their own.

"This Gully will be no more a *Badnaam Gully.* Throw this woman out from here."

There were women of NGOs as well. The scene was epic chaos.

She opened the door and came out like everything was finished. Her dupatta at the side slipped. She took steps towards the body, this time not wrapped in the tricolour, yet it is a body of a man working in the 'Central Board of Investigation.'

She wailed in agony. It was her son who hadn't been able to stand against the firing. In the end, the team of terrorists had thrown a loaded RDX.

Everything stopped. The people bid her salute. Finally, she was known as the mother of 'Martyr Bhuttar'. At that moment, everyone had tears in their eyes. Even her family members were standing there to embrace her. She stood, wiped her tears, and said, "This is my life, my place. I left Punjab ages ago. After Ranjit, nothing is left for me there."

She looked at that woman who had created chaos. "I belong to this *Badnaam Gully*."

Sixteen

THE UNLOCKING

The rainfall that day made Ankita realise that one needs to dictate one's mind rather than it letting it dictate them. The mind is always the prey of thoughts and is barely ready to let patience spread across. That was the day she made the same mistake. A choice can ruin all; was she still lucky enough?

The entire world was shut. It was 2020, the year when turning on the news channel would shackle your soul. The same was happening to her. She was sinking with grief and couldn't find anything to keep herself sane. There was sadness everywhere. She tried to read more and more but could not keep herself indulged in words for the first ever time in her life. She could not embrace words anymore. She got married four months ago; this pandemic was there as per the resources, but it wasn't too close. So, since her wedding, she was attending dinners, parties, family meets, and what-not. She always had a problem that her husband didn't spare time for her. The whole day would pass by. She couldn't call him until it was urgent. Seems funny, but gathering the entire experience of newlywed, she had made a mistake.

****

"I hear voices in the night. Rohit, could you and Ankita please come to my place for a few days until I figure out if this is really in my head?"

"Look, Simona, I never said all this isn't true. You aren't lying. Believe me, such things are possible. This could be due to the stress you are taking because of Udit. I know you can't forget all that. Believe me, it's not worth it. He won't do anything. Let us plan something to let him fall into the trap as he did. Online dating, huh… you discussed everything with me being your friend but this."

****

The phone pinged sequentially. The WhatsApp messages popped. "There?" "Listen?" "It's important…"

"Rohit?" Ankita called out as he was in the shower. "Your phone. It was a missed call. I guess someone is dying for you. So many messages, Mr. GM," she peeped into the bathroom.

"Ha-ha."

"I'm dying for this," she winked while teasing her husband.

Her hands went straight to his phone, but she didn't open the messages, just gazed through the read receipts. Five unread messages. The top one read, "What should I do with the nudes?"

She seemed to have fallen into the pit of the earth, like the thunder had fallen like Ekta Kapoor's K-series climax. Nevertheless, it was something she had always been frightened of!

****

"He is indeed married to me, and that's what kills you. I remember you didn't have a smile on our wedding day."

"No… Leave me," she replied, howling. "We are friends. What did I do?"

"This is for snatching my husband from me."

"Rohit is yours. He loves you, Ankita. Damn it," she said, half pleading and in half confusion.

"Shut up. Don't call our names with your dirty mouth," she said while hurting her fingers with a blade and pulling her hair.

Simona screamed in pain. She tried to push her away, but every effort was in vain. Ankita was behaving like a hurt tigress, full of power and rage.

It was raining rigorously outside. Simona's eyes were watered with physical pain and Ankita's with emotion. What was God up to? Something really bad was going to happen tonight.

****

Two days after returning from their honeymoon, it was Simona's birthday bash. Simona was their common friend from college. Rohit, Simona, and Ankita had been best friends. The difference was that Ankita was the quiet one, and the other two were bandits, not just humorous but also little bullies. Those were just college things. Or maybe…

"Rohit, what should I wear tonight? The black lacy one or the long red dress?"

"Wear the red one."

"Cool!" she winked.

She got ready, and Rohit called Simona. They talked for almost half an hour, laughing, discussing things. Ankita stood there for Rohit to take notice. But he was busy discussing the execution of the party.

Rohit came out after a while in a dashing black satin shirt and black trousers.

"Let's go."

"Mhm."

He stepped back to apply his body-mist. He smelled divine.

Ankita teased him in the car. He, too, like a teenager, parked the car in the distance and started kissing her.

"You look stunning! I feel like I'm drunk on you," she giggled.

His hands were all over her back.

"Okay, okay, aren't we getting late?"

"Mhm… just a while." He had a victorious look on his face.

"What?" she enquired.

"Nothing."

****

At the entrance, she walked as if on the aisle of Miss Universe. Everyone was giggling, looking her up and down, wondering why on earth she was wearing that.

"It isn't a fancy dress."

"Oh, you are the spotlight, Ankita. Newlywed indeed. Red dress, *Chooda*."

She was not comfortable with the compliments. An hour passed; it was cake-cutting time. She stepped on something, and a squelching sound came. There was a tail stuck with many sticky notes on it, with self-centric questions on it.

"How am I looking?"

"Isn't this red dress gorgeous?"

"How is my make-up?"

She felt embarrassed. She ran out of the party, then and there, without creating a scene.

"Ankita, stop. Anku, stop!"

"Anku, Anku," both Simona and Rohit followed her.

She stopped and turned with tears in her eyes.

"We are no longer in college, Rohit, where one friend out of the three is used for leg-pulling or bullying. I am your wife now. Enough!"

She took an auto and left.

"Did we hurt her this time?" they wondered.

****

Ankita reached home crying, removed her dress, remembering the doing of her own husband. Simona, since their college days, had always beguiled Rohit for such things. Now, she must stay away. She cried herself to sleep. Rohit came home late, and she didn't even ask why. When the next day arrived, the previous night's incident vanished. She seems to have forgotten the episode. Or had she?

****

Rohit got into his car, and his phone started ringing.

"Hello, yup, Simona."

"Could you just drop by my house?"

"Right now? Simona, I got free early today. I thought of surprising Ankita and taking her for dinner."

"It can't wait, Rohit. I am having hallucinations. I'm stressed. Until I am under the spell of medicines, I am fine, but after that, it's suffocating."

"You have to forget the incident. Udit is over now. Move on!"

"No, it isn't over. I see him every day. He talks to me, blackmailing me with my pictures. Last night, he almost mailed the pictures to my colleagues. I'll be finished, Rohit."

"Simona, it is nothing like that. I was with you, I am with you, my friend. He is behind bars. He won't be able to touch you. Wait, I'll come for a while."

Rohit reached and was awestruck to see Simona's condition.

"I am begging you, Rohit, could you and Ankita move in with me for a few months? I'll be fine."

****

Those fifteen days were a test for Ankita. Whom could she believe?

When Rohit came four days ago from the office having high fever demanding to be immediately isolated, Ankita never expected he would be infected along with Simona.

Simona and Rohit must have met a few days ago, and now they were meeting covertly. They got sick together, they made fun of Ankita, and then they would say she thought too much!

Early the same morning, Ankita's phone was ringing. It was Simona. She let it ring. When she called again, Ankita picked up.

"Is Rohit fine now?"

"Yeah, he is. What happened?"

"I tested positive yesterday."

"What? Oh god." Ankita didn't feel bad, though. She only felt intensifying rage. She hated Simona. She started weeping and disconnected.

****

It was thundering.

No one could hear Simona's cries. Ankita was not leaving any chance of hurting her.

Ankita's phone rang just then. It was Rohit.

"Where are you, damn it?"

"I'm finishing an unfinished project."

"What? What project? Where are you?"

Before she could hang up, he heard cries.

Rohit was getting restless. He tried Simona, but she didn't answer.

"See, my husband is now trying you instead of finding his wife. He is trying his girlfriend. You both have been fooling me around since college. Why didn't you both get married? Even after marriage, you both plan to bully me every now and then as if I'm a toy without feelings. You sent him your nudes when he was my husband. What a shame."

"What?" Simona in a perplexed shrug. "No, my friend."

"Shut up… I said shut up. Do not call me your friend."

Half knowledge was treacherous.

"Believe me!" she cried. "It's my fault."

"Yes, indeed. You'll have to pay for it."

She slashed the knife on the backside of her hand. Simona cried, unstoppably, uncontrollably, and once more. She couldn't stop herself and puked blood. She was traumatised seeing her best friend turn into a murderer.

Just then, the doorbell rang. She looked at the security camera. It was Rohit, drenched in the rain; his hands at the back; shivering. She talked to Simona.

"See, your lover finally found us. You won't get him in this life, I tell you."

Ten minutes later, Rohit barged into the room where Simona was tied. He strolled each and every corner before finally reaching Simona. He came close and stabbed her with all his efforts. Once, twice, thrice!

He got up and ran towards the door where Ankita was struggling to breathe. Blood ran ruthlessly from the left side of her neck.

"Oho, tch… tch… tch… This is what you did to me. My life had been suffocating ever since I married you. And then, this mad Simona. You both are, no, no, no, were extremes. You loved unlocking my phone and checking my messages. However, I never lied to you; it was just something I hid from you for a few days. I had liked Simona in college. She had never considered me as more than a friend. So, I got married to you, in order to maintain our group. You are a psycho. I can't handle you. So, I finally found the love of my life. I'll get married once this mess is cleared."

"Who…? Wh…?"

"Oh, don't struggle so much. In the last time of yours, pray to God. You'll find solace in heaven. I'll still answer, though. It is my colleague, Meeta. She doesn't know about this plan at all. For her, like everyone else, this would be an open-and-shut case. A psycho wife killed a friend with whom she was apprehensive of her husband having an extra-marital affair. The friend, in self-defence, stabbed the knife in the sensitive area. She couldn't bear it and died herself, too. The camera recordings, I'll take care of, my love."

She breathed her last and shut her eyes forever.

Seventeen

CONFINED TO THE PAST

A restless commotion was brewing. She started groaning. This time, Utkarsh didn't take much time to get acquainted with his wife's pain. He knew this after all. This was happening for the 4th time in a row. She started to haul whimsically. She touched herself down, and it was all wet in sadness. The good news was, no more waiting to be held in her arms. Utkarsh banged his knuckles on the side walls.

"Doctor, is she okay?"

"Yeah... if you ask physically. Although it's her 4th time in a row, Dr. Purvi is a steel woman with a heart of gold. Will you just come with me?" Dr. Aradhna gestured to Utkarsh to follow her.

She had a sonography report a day ago. Everything was smooth, then what happened this time?

There weren't any complications. But Dr. Purvi was anxious after seeing the baby moments.

"Oh, she didn't mention the sonography."

"Um, I don't know!"

****

It was a day of beautiful vibes. Purvi sipped her coffee and let the petrichor sink into her nerves. Hardly did she get such afternoons of tranquillity.

She opened a maternity novel written by her friend, which described her rollercoaster journey of pregnancy.

"I didn't expect to be expected," it read.

"Aha… my baby is indulged in some drama," Utkarsh clapped her hand. "The cover picture and the title suit the scenario."

"Um, I think, as the quick test says, yet no excitement till I get the confirmation. I'll get it by tomorrow. I submitted my sample to get confirmed."

Oh, come on." Utkarsh feigned all the sanity in a go. He was dancing like a clown and hugged Purvi on this statement.

She was always on her toes to work for humanity. A great doctor. Everyone wanted her to treat their loved ones. People built trust in her the moment she came into the picture. They said she had magic in her hands apart from the knowledge of science.

Her phone rang, and she picked up.

"Hello."

On the other side, there was a sound of a new-born mulling, gurgling, whistling.

"Hello? Who's this?"

The sound was now louder.

"Hello… hello… hello… What a terrible prank is this?" she slammed the receiver as though she woke from a bad dream. She was drenched in sweat. Utkarsh was in front of her, consoling her.

"Baby, we can't do anything. If it's not meant to be, we can't say anything. I can thank God that my Purvi is safe. You are fine. It is happening for the fourth time and would be a really difficult time for both of us, for mom and dad, too."

"Oh, please!" She swatted his hand away and manoeuvred to the next room.

****

Purvi locked and double-checked the locks before going back to the room to sleep. This was her ritual when she got to sleep during normal hours. Due to the miscarriage, the senior doctor asked her to take rest for a week. Though she wanted to jump on to join the service back asap, the family and everyone suggested that she take good rest.

She started to tickle Utkarsh. Utkarsh laid his hand for Purvi to lie her head on it. Purvi seemed to be on some different tangent.

She started to create some sounds to arouse Utkarsh, but he patted her and mentioned her health scenario.

"You don't understand, Utkarsh."

"What don't I understand? What is the hurry? You are not fit for all this."

"Oh, really? Who told you?" interrogated Purvi.

"It is obvious."

"I want a child," she said exasperatedly.

"We will if fate wills it. It doesn't mean you get pressurised by this."

"Utkarsh, we would have a son by now who would be four by this year's end."

"Ha-ha, yes, but a daughter."

"Why? It has to be a son. Each time our luck wasn't on our side, we had a daughter. Did we do such bad deeds that God is cursing us like this? People say parents who are blessed with daughters have done some extra good deeds in their past lives. But is our fate such that they came this near just to leave us childless?"

She turned her face towards the wall. Utkarsh kept on talking, which she ignored and sank to sleep.

****

Everywhere in the house, there was pomp and zeal. The house was lit with the best of seasonal flowers. Purvi and Utkarsh were busy receiving the guests. The pandit had started the ritual of the name-giving ceremony. The family was blessed with a baby boy. After the basic norms, the pandit asked to bring the boy for the final call.

Purvi stood up to fetch the boy from the side by the cot. The baby was sleeping. She carefully wrapped her arms around him. The baby seemed to be still without any activity. Purvi called him by the name the new parents gave him when they first held him in their arms. The grandparents came forward, and Purvi pulled down the *Mulmul* cloth in which the boy was wrapped. All she could see were her hands covered in blood. She screamed deafeningly. The zeal in the house turned into mourning. No one knew what curse this next moment brought into their lives.

She was hurling until she finally woke up from this dreadful dream.

"What happened, Purvi?"

"I lost my baby boy even after he was in my arms," she cried

"What?"

"He was just here in my hands," she gestured as carrying a baby in her hands.

"It was just a dream. It was just a dream," he repeated.

"No, I had him here."

Utkarsh shook Purvi's shoulder to bring her back from the trauma.

She cried till the black clouds over her eyes settled to sleep. While sleeping, she held Utkarsh's hands tightly.

****

The next morning, she finally got ready for the hospital as she seemed to be fine to get back.

She found a letter on the porch. She opened it, and the handwriting was like a child who had recently started scribbling. "I know your escapades already. Where will you go, Mumma? Daddy will know this all very soon," she read.

She crumbled the letter but did not throw it. Instead, she put it inside her handbag. She was restless since she read the letter.

There was a bang on her table. So loud that she was enervated.

"What is this, Anubha?" She screamed at Anubha. Anubha was Purvi's colleague and a very good friend.

"Where are you lost? The lines on your forehead are too deep. What's the matter?"

"N... n... nothing."

"Oh, come on!"

"Nothing, Anubha, don't prick me again and again."

"Oh... okay. I'll leave you alone for now. I just came to check on you. Today, Dr. Bhasin told me to check on the footfall. You'll get to dive into work slowly. Don't make your first day too hectic. Leave early today," Anubha mentioned with concern. "By the way, many of your patients called to check in on you. Your patients love you."

"Anubha, could you do me a small favour?"

"Um, tell, all... of me to all... of you…" she started singing the song by John Legend.

"Shut up, you cheesy girl. *Uske naam mai hi legend hai* (The legend is in his name itself)," muttered Purvi, turning a little uncomfortable with what she just said.

"Just like you, Mummy," something echoed, and there was a blackout for a jiffy.

"Arey, that's fine, *yaara* (friend)."

"Just bring my handbag from the counter. I was checking the register in the morning and left it there."

"Okay-dokay…."

Anubha went to the entry counter with lightning speed and bumped into some guy.

It wasn't a Bollywood shot, just all the things from Purvi's bag were now scattered on the floor. She was shocked for a while and quickly put the belongings inside the bag. She handed over the bag to Purvi without mentioning the Bollywood story.

****

For the past few days, Purvi seemed to be frightened whenever the landline or the doorbell rang.

She was sipping a warm cup of coffee in the evening. Utkarsh was stuck at work and called up for being late. The evening suddenly turned dark outside, as if the thunder had emerged to take away all the pain. Purvi called her mother-in-law so that she wouldn't feel alone. She had a long chat with her that evening, until the call was interrupted by another call. The person didn't wait. He called four times in a row until she was forced to disconnect her mother's call to attend this impulsive one.

"Why did you do this to us?" someone said in a hushed tone.

"Who is this?"

"You'll pay for this," came another statement that made her heart pound a little more.

She screamed and cut the call. She couldn't stand to cook the meal that evening. The call was from an unknown number. That lady cursed her to death.

****

"Hey, hi."

"Why did you call me like this?"

"Hi, Utkarsh. Sit, please."

"Yes, but I can't leave Purvi alone for hours. She is still having disturbing thoughts."

"Yes, indeed, because her pot of lies is overflowing now."

"What are you saying?"

"Um," Anubha rolled her eyes. "You'll be upset to know that your wife is cheating on you."

"What the hell? Just because I am not saying anything, that doesn't mean you have the right to utter anything about my wife."

"See this!" she banged an almost empty medicine packet on the table in front of Utkarsh.

Utkarsh lifted the medicine cover, "what is this?"

"Read!"

"Mifeprex. Where did you get this?"

"Purvi's bag."

"What?"

"She has been playing with everyone's emotions since the beginning. I even checked with Dr. Aradhna. She wasn't happy after the sonography. Though it is not allowed to be revealed, because I'm a staff member, she told me that it was a girl in the womb. When Dr. Aradhna inquired, she said no matter what, baby girls will never be welcomed."

That sowed a seed of anger in him, which would blast like a volcano. Disheartened, he got into his car. He called on the home landline. No one picked even after the third missed call.

Many questions were forming a tornado inside him that evening. He reached home with a furious scowl and banged the door with all the strength left in him. To which, when it wasn't open ajar for him, he broke in and found Purvi laid on a shattered table glass, covered with blood. He lifted her and went to the hospital.

****

Purvi was born to a Bengali litterateur. Her mother was a housewife but used to stitch designer clothes. She had a bountiful childhood until the doomsday of the Chakravarty family. It was the time when she was returning home from high school and received the last call from her Maa. She inquired, "How long will it take you to be back?" before their house was set on fire.

Purvi's father was a courageous, big-mouthed author and penned every problem of society in his writings. It wasn't a time of blogs or online exposure, so people were still into reading newspaper columns and books. This time he made the mistake of confronting someone so powerful: a high-profile rape case. He used the real names of the people involved and dragged them into a big controversy, to which many people trolled him as a publicity stunt of an author. Although he was right, his voice was taken for granted. In fact, his house, his wife, everything was burnt to ashes.

Purvi stood there, watching everything burn in front of her eyes. For the rest of her life, she struggled to arrange a smile on her face for the next time when the lamps went off, and it was dark.

She left Bengal and came to Delhi. She was fortunate that her father trusted her daughter and had secured her education already. Even after being an orphan, she completed her medical studies. While completing studies, she met Utkarsh through a common friend. She didn't hide anything from him. Utkarsh embraced her for what she was.

****

Purvi was gaining consciousness now. The nurse went outside to seek the doctor.

After the examination, she looked here and there for her husband. Utkarsh entered with gloom on his face.

"Why did you do this to me?"

"I was scared."

"But for what?" inquired Utkarsh. "You had me. I never brought up the past. I just loved you the way you are. Then why? Why?" he asked, gritting his teeth in anger.

"I had a bad time without my parents. This world is not a good place for women. I wanted a boy, but every time, it was a girl," she cried loudly. "I didn't want her to suffer like me if something happened to us."

"Damn! Who allowed you to do this to me? Those were my daughters you took away from me. You bitch! And you still have the guts to speak such rubbish. Yes, life is unpredictable. Still, before sunset, we humans always wish for the sunlight for ourselves. Why did the Lord even waste his clay on you?"

"No, Utkarsh, I realised it late until the souls started haunting me. I never wanted to face you like this. I tried taking my own life. God wanted this. I am so sorry."

"Some mistakes are never forgiven, Purvi. You must have left the past behind and embraced the overwhelming present and future. I had a lot of dreams for us as a family. You ruined everything. No one can destroy iron, but its own rust can! And you did the same."

There was a knock on the door. A policeman was standing at the porch of the hospital room. They had come for Purvi's statement.

"She must be given the taste of confinement forever," uttered Utkarsh in a cursing tone, cupping his face inside his palms.

Eighteen

THE END OF THE STORY WHICH NEVER BEGAN

Meera was on her balcony, reading "Le Balcon" by Jean Genet. She was indulged in her play when someone called her.

"Hey, you dropped a paper."

She looked at the ground and found a slip with a phone number written on it. She remembered that the number was special, so special, that she quickly folded it back and hid between the yellow and dull pages of the play she was reading.

"What happened? Did I disturb you?"

"Who are you?" she asked.

"Arey, um, I am just inquiring. A beautiful lady with a book in her hand. Reading a love story. Why a love story?"

"It's a play," she grinned. *The voice seems so melodious,* she thought.

She couldn't see the face, just hear the voice due to the unequal extension of the balconies. Her balcony was vastly extended than his.

****

Two days ago, Meera got down just to buy fresh vegetables as this pandemic was at its peak and everyone in the society almost stopped interacting with each other. Without even stepping out, there was news of five deaths on the RWA WhatsApp group.

Everyone was scared. People had begun washing everything from floors to lentils packet with Lizol and Dettol hand wash. While coming back, she checked the letterbox. It was empty. After a few steps, she checked her hand, and some number with a ball pen was written on it. It seems to be fading, to which she ran home to rewrite it somewhere. She didn't remember why she wrote the number and to whom it belonged.

****

Meera was sipping tea in her balcony, humming tunes.

"Hey, Meera. Could you help me cook some butter chicken? For the last five days, I smelled the aromatic tempering of vegetables and chicken. You seem to be a brilliant cook."

"Are you following me day and night?" Meera confusingly enquired. "Without even seeing me?"

"Hey, I don't need to see you to adore you. Your voice seems to be the music to my ears. God knows what will happen if I see you. *Waise* (by the way), the house belongs to my distant uncle, and I am here just to complete my quarantine. I came here with my dad, though my dad is feeble due to certain health issues."

"I understand. This period is tough for all of us. Hope, he will be fine soon," Meera said with a smile.

"Thanks."

"So, butter chicken? Don't worry, I'll cook for you, and you just taste it."

"Um, okay!"

She cooked butter chicken that day. She used the rope to slide a bowl on the floor below them so that the new guy could have it.

Every evening since then, Raahi played guitar, and she listened to it. Sometimes she read, sometimes they just exchanged information about themselves and their families.

"You know what? We both got negative test results, but they say we still have to complete the quarantine period before going back, as sometimes these test reports aren't authentic and don't nicely catch the virus. Today is just the 5th day. Tomorrow, once again, we will just give the samples and then we are free to go to our house. I think Meera, I will become a refugee here at my uncle's place so that I can meet you, even if in the abstract! Once I am tested negative again, I'll go back to my family in Dwarka."

"We will meet once things calm down."

"By the way, the butter chicken was yummy."

"You want the same once again?" Meera asked excitedly.

"Um, yeah. why not?"

****

"Butter chicken again? You aren't just cooking butter chicken. Tell me, what is it?" Sneha asked, irritated.

"You are an overthinker. I'm not." .

"Look who's talking," Sneha mocked her.

"Ugh." Meera was irritated.

She just received her order of French chicken, from fresh to home, while the rest of the preparations were in time.

"Maa, I understand you are tired, but I can't eat this every day. That, too, when this is about something not good."

Sneha wasn't as polite. "The isolation had finally driven her looney," she said.

Her mother muttered, "Shut up, Sneha!"

While she was cooking his favourite butter chicken, she thought the window of his room would directly summon him, and he would drive to her through the aroma. The case wasn't the same. All the time she was cooking, she was thinking about him, his build, his hair, his eyes.

The next moment turned her life upside down. Her father entered the house shouting, "I saved you, but I couldn't save poor Mr. Chhabra."

"What happened, Papa?"

His eyes flashed with anger. "It's all their fault. Those NRIs."

Meera's heart went cold, "Who?"

"The *baap-beta* from the U.S. who wanted to be quarantined upstairs. I objected to RWA, but they never came here. Otherwise, today, it could have been your mother or me. When Mr. Chaabra died of corona, the same evening their test results came, and they both were tested positive."

Those words stabbed Meera's chest. She left everything and ran downstairs. Her father was shouting, "Meera! Meera!"

She didn't listen. She just said, "He needs me." She went and banged on the door.

"Meera, this house has been deserted since 2012. The house has been sealed since 2012."

From the side balcony, Sneha saw the stale butter chicken she dropped using a rope. It was her love or her chronic illness, 'schizophrenia,' that hit her again, since she found that contact number. She just could not take her eyes off from the number plate 301.

She came down musing on a poem of hers which she had written in her early college days.

"She can toss my little heart in the heat in a pan

The world sputters and sizzles

With a flick of her hand

She has cast her spell, and now I can't stay far" in her book "Le Balcon."

Their love was nothing. It was just in her mind, which was the result of her endless torment.

Nineteen

A SEED SOWN, A STAND TAKEN

The distorted rubber chappals were wet, in which Sagarika's feet hurt while walking. Still, she hardly bothered about the pain and always dabbled in still water wherever she saw it. Today was such a day. The weather suddenly changed to something cooler, and it had drizzled a while ago. Now, the leaves were covered with tiny droplets. One would need a magnifying glass to enlarge the beauty.

"Saagu…" came a feeble yet hoarse voice.

"Saagu…"

Just as Sagarika rushed inside, Mahira vomited. She threw up everything she had just eaten. Her body was now a container that had numerous holes. It could retain nothing. She even had nebulous vision nowadays.

"Jiji (sister), you'll be fine," Sagarika sad, consoling Mahika.

The darker shades were evident under her eyes.

****

He whistled thrice in an odd tone.

Mahira sped up a little. It was Jason again, the guy she hated in every aspect.

While briskly walking, he was following her, and she had a hazy recall of the bus incident that happened a week ago.

****

She got on the bus one stop before. Mahira was known for being extra vigilant in managing things, but the bus was crowded, and Jason was standing just behind her. He found this a perfect opportunity to squeeze her extra elevated breasts. She found it difficult to accept the reality that the boobs she had could be a dream of some other girl. When he did it, she could not scream, rathe just tried to prevent it with her hands, but failed. He squeezed it for a good two minutes, and she thought it was her fault that she was different, and her body was wrong that it always dragged the pervert's attention. She wailed so hard that night that even her pillow had completely drenched.

****

She sped up and stumbled twice and could not stop the pervert chasing her. In fact, she found it embarrassing to run at full speed and make the extra luggage wobble more and let that pervert pass another demeaning comment.

He came closer, got a hold of her, touched her, squeezed the boobs to his pleasure, and left. She was just nineteen at that time. In the last year of her teens, she collected dismaying memories because of her zaftig body part.

"Ma, I want to tell you something."

"Yes?" her mother asked, disinterested.

"Ma, someone is following me everywhere," she sobbed.

"Didn't I tell you to wear full-length clothes and not these fancy dresses?" her mother taunted. She looked at her below knees yellow dress.

Is maa, right? Is this the reason and not the boobs?

The next day, she gave away the mere dresses she possessed.

"Do we have a money tree? Don't you dare buy such horrendous dresses in life, ever. Such things attract boys with rake thoughts," her ma uttered. That night, Mahira thought a small change would be enough to welcome a drastic change in her life. She slept in tranquillity even after that chasing incident.

****

Today when he did the same on the bus, she could not stop herself. She got up and called Sagarika, her maid and good friend. Sagarika was a fourteen-year-old girl, busy enjoying her life, and least worried for tomorrow.

"Do you want a new slipper?" asked Mahira.

"Um, do you have pocket money?"

"What?"

"I am asking because I can't go to school now as I am working a full day at your place. Could you buy me some books so that I can study at night?"

Mahira was happy with the way she asked her this.

"Though I am working full-time, Jiji, My Mumma knows what you are paying me. She takes everything, and your Mumma always gives me leftovers, old clothes, miscellaneous things. I want books. I want to study."

Mahira broke her piggy bank and gave her a thousand rupees. She knew she would get a tight slap for doing this but decided to hide the reality of how she used this money. She said that she needed some money for a school farewell, where she had the least amount of will to go. She had to get ready and walk on the aisle facing this guy, Jason. She had no strength.

****

The tiny effort of Mahira had made Sagarika her best friend. She was now mostly keeping herself inside the four walls, and her parents were not worried about her behaviour. But Sagarika knew everything. She not only consoled her but also asked her to take a stand for herself, to which she said her parents would render her the culprit like always. She at least needed someone to back her.

"I better leave my studies, too."

"What? Jiji, I'll never let that happen," assured Sagarika.

It was Sagarika's 11th standard exam, and she was preparing her assignments. She was studying under streetlamps, sitting on the terrace. She suddenly heard a thud as if something broke. She got up and ran from where the sound came.

Mahira was locked in the washroom, and Sagarika knew the sound came from in there. The tap was running, yet the panting was audible. She urgently fetched Mahira's parents.

They both entered her room, rubbing their eyes.

"What happened?" both inquired.

"Jiji is not okay. She is crying. She is locked. Something fell down."

"Oh no, did she break that crystal showpiece you just bought?"

"Shut up. Let me check," muttered her father.

Somehow, they managed to bring her out; that's when she announced that she had some problem.

After that day, nothing was normal for her. Her devastated soul was now inside a body that hurt a lot. The reports announced that she had cancer and needed surgery. They would have to extract both her breasts as it had spread all over. If not done, then she would be soon gone forever.

****

While Sagarika was enjoying the beautiful weather, Mahira was struggling and gasping hard. Today, Sagarika appeared for her 12th exam. She was eighteen now. Four years had passed, a lot had changed for Sagarika, but Mahira, on the other hand, suffered each day. Earlier, because of a bad guy, and now this disease.

Mahira's small effort made Sagarika's life heaven, yet Mahira never got what she deserved. She wasn't a bad person. She always listened to her parents, even after they always failed to understand their daughter. Meanwhile, these years, Jason also got married and had his family, although that didn't change him. Till last year, he did squeeze her whenever he got the chance. Mahira coiled, sans utter, shout, or cry.

****

Jason was in a full mood to enjoy the weather today. Normally, a little rain made the surroundings humid, but today was different. It was cold, and that made Jason want to drink. He was a chain smoker too. It was already on his fourth peg and still sober. He had the capacity of a tanker.

****

A whole year had passed. She was sipping her juice, facing a window that remained shut.

This time when Sagarika helped her maintain balance, she suddenly turned red with rage, letting out all her pent-up anger.

"Stop it, Jiji. Today, I will not take pity on you. It's your mistake. I told you a number of times. It's you who has to back yourself up. No one else will do it. You never listen to me. That pervert ruined your teenage. And this cancer took away everything. This chemo made you feeble more than before. You can't just stay like this. Kill yourself! It's much better. I am sick of taking care of a dead body. Yeah, you heard it right! Have you ever seen me like this? What do I have? Not even a home. I decided to continue my studies. You definitely emerged as an angel, but would it be possible if I never chose to be like that? The answer is no. In this brutal world, no one will help you if you don't help yourself. Even this cancer could not take your life, yet you have no right to live." She banged the door and left.

She was anxious, though, as she repeated the same more than she had to.

Would Mahira be okay?

After ten minutes, when there was nothing to hear, Sagarika thought of going inside and checking on Mahira. But right on cue, Mahira came out with a bare chest where her stitches were evident. She took Sagarika with her. Everyone's jaws dropped while seeing such a shameless woman. No top? Had she gone nuts? Her parents approached her to prevent her from creating any scene.

Jason might already be down with more than 7-8 pegs, and might have vomited as well, yet continued.

When he was downing another peg, his doorbell rang. He didn't have any strength, so his wife opened the door. Mahira walked inside and slapped him once, twice, thrice. That was enough to make him sober again.

"You bitch! What is this? Where are your clothes? You are looking awful. I'll puke again."

She laughed and uttered, "You loved my chest a lot, right?"

While everyone looked at the scene, her parents tried to drag her out.

"Stay away! You have no right to touch me. When I wanted you, I didn't have you, and today, I don't need you," she declared, her voice placed with confidence.

Her mother was precise about disowning her.

She slapped him once again, making his hand touch the surface. He actually puked. She removed the scarf too. The chemo made her look symmetrical with two craters on her chest, where there used to be an elevated structure, good enough to draw everyone's attention.

That moment, she turned her sight everywhere. Paper cups, cigarette butts, vomit. There were even a couple of broken flowerpots, the mud spilling out, oddly angled flowers with broken stems. And because it was all so depressing, the overturned plastic chairs and food half-eaten on Styrofoam plates, she knew that she would have to make up her mind about it all. Did she really want to be here?

After all those years of suffering, she decided to live for herself and do something. She came out of a long depression and worked for the well-being of girls fighting cancer. She left her parents, too, but always kept in touch with Sagarika. Life was so vicious, and attachments were often unwelcomed.

Today, she was on television, being honoured for her deeds by the Prime Minister.

There, she just said, "After all this, I have just one thing to say. If you don't stand up for yourself, no one else will!"

Twenty

TWELVE RUPEES

It was the midsummer of 1987. Unnati had just graduated with her first degree and had come home with an enlightened smile.

"Papa," she summoned when her father was carving the tiny house plants he loved. With tiny scissors and an equally tiny spray water bottle.

"*Hanji, puttar* (Yes, kiddo)?"

"Papa, I topped the class!"

"*Oye hoye, main sadqe jawan!* (Oh, la la, I'm in awe!)" he seemed happier than her.

He was jumping like a monkey to celebrate his daughter's victory as his life had not been that much of a celebration. He had lost his wife and his younger son in an accident when they were returning from their maternal house. Their bus had slipped into the river, where not even their bodies were retrieved. He saw his daughter's hard work to fidget between chores and studies as he lost almost all the interest to live a life king size. He searched his pockets where he could find only twelve rupees, which he presented to his daughter as a gift of a lifetime.

"I know you are wise, *puttar*. But I learned a lesson that life is unpredictable, that when you least expect it, it may give you the highest bump, which might shatter your entire life. And money is something that is even more important, as without it you will not be able to buy love for your family."

"It's not like that, papa. See, I know how much you love me even after what has happened. When Ma and Bhaiya left, everyone around us was celebrating."

"No, *beta*, people are curious and jealous only for those things which they cannot easily have. Where curiosity carves you, jealousy starves you in the end."

"I get it, papa."

"The drama reaches to draw the veils. So, both of you proceed to your respective works," uttered Sharda, Unnati's aunt.

Sharda was Unnati's father's elder brother's wife. She took hold of the entire house after Unnati's mother's demise, and her husband was the sole navigator of the business when it was actually established by Unnati's parents.

Unnati lost the only supporter in her life as his father was depressed after the incident. Unnati silently slid the money into her pocket, but she remembered the teaching of her father.

****

The year 1989.

It was a foggy winter, and Unnati was under the shed where she was gathering the clothes that were drenched in dew. The clothes were as cold as her uncle and aunt's hearts. She never realised that the last one and a half years had passed in such haste, and before she could recall the last touch of her father, her aunt summoned her.

"Unnati! Where are you? I asked you to bring the clothes, not to start the construction of your dream house," she taunted.

She ran downstairs and reached their dry balcony to start the blower for the clothes. Delhi winters were difficult for everyone.

She was lost in thought. The blower started covering all the voices surrounding it as it was as old as her paternal aunt's thought process. Besides, she was rapping. The beats, rap, and blower were an utmost sight and desirable music to anyone.

There was some melange screaming, hushing, grinding that could be heard from a distance that distracted Unnati from her thoughts, and just then, the cursing words were breaking in.

"Yes, she is a load for me," cursed Pratap, Unnati's uncle.

"B... bu... but it wasn't her fault. I did to date, as you said, but now it's not my cup of tea. You at least see your own son. Our own Mayank is now dependent on us even for peeing. He had that attack that left him pauperised from any happiness he deserved. Don't you think it is the Karma of what we did to her? I mean, if we had supported her after her father's haemorrhage, she would have completed her master's degree and maybe further studies. She has talent," sighed Sharda.

"It wasn't a haemorrhage," grinned Pratap.

"What? Then?"

Pratap gave a sly smile that described his whereabouts and criminal activities in his own household. He pushed himself further by mentioning, "She has to marry that middle-aged man in order to pay me what I spent on her after her father's death. I am not here to do charity."

Sharda fell on a side couch, destitute of any phrase or emotion. She, till date, thought that she was helping her husband, and now she felt forlorn of any relation around her.

There was a sudden thud from a distance. Sharda and Pratap ran towards the sound. They came across a puddle of spilled water and a broken blower kissing the ground, still creating ruckus sounds. There was no sign of Unnati. Pratap followed her to some extent, but today, she was a girl on fire. After a few hours, there was no sign of her. Her uncle came back home to see Sharda already setting herself on fire. When he spilled water, there were almost 2nd degree burns. She survived with burn marks all over, which she carried as her repentance.

****

February 1990

Today, after two months, Sharda seemed to be happy, as if some sort of divine feeling had surrounded her. Pratap faced a huge loss in business, regarding his deal of getting his niece married to that middle-aged man. Moreover, he let other contracts slip from his hands in front of his eyes. Pratap, after the accident, lost interest in his wife. She was nothing but a quiet living being around him.

****

The train just left, and Unnati could not climb it as today her attire was torn from the side. Her part was visible, and the reason why she turned tail and took the woods was to set her dignity intact. Her age was not of such twisted twirls. She was such a brilliant girl who deserved all the happiness. She wished every morning that her parents would be beside her, but life was not even an inch like this.

The graduated girl was now begging on the local train of Mumbai after the day she burnt down her paternal home. After not getting refuge from any maternal home, the only thing she could do was to flee to some other part of the country where no one knew her, covered in dirt, with just that ten rupees note and two rupees coin that she had from her father.

****

"How fast can you sing? Are these your self-written ones? I

haven't heard any of these before. I often hear these from you," a stranger with a spark in his eyes inquired.

"Um… I write these. I sleep here only. This is my house," she pointed towards a tattered, covered tent with bare neatness.

"You sing brilliantly. Do you know how to rap in different ways?"

"Yeah, I do. I had sung a few songs, but those aren't with me now. I left that life and those dreams behind. Once I had a home, but now, I have nothing," Unnati bitterly chuckled.

"You have everything," the stranger smiled and left.

****

Rishabh, the stranger, pondered a lot and tried to discover if he had heard a similar voice before.

How come it is possible to have this feeling for someone who is just a beggar? No, she has something. I must try to find out.

****

Rishabh was on a school trip where all the boys were in a fun mood and listening to B-grade dialogues from scenes of weird movies. Just then, in one of his friends' Walkman, he heard a beautiful rap. Everyone was astonished to hear such a melodious voice.

"Who is this rapper?"

"*Yaar*, she is such a queen," his friend mentioned that his cousin had given him the cassette, saying it's his paternal sister.

Rishabh recalled the incident. He took out his phone and called his friend.

"Hello? Yes, Karthik?"

"Hmmm," he opened his eyes.

"Who is that cousin of yours who gave you that CD?"

"What cousin? What are you talking about, Rishabh? It is past two. Please sleep. We will talk tomorrow."

"No, I want to know! I think I know that girl. She is living in rags. We must help her."

"Hein? My cousin's sister is dead," he said. "How can you find someone you don't even ever see or hear?"

"I don't know. I just want to help her. Okay, I'll try to find out tomorrow. Please."

"Okay."

****

Mayank was near the landline when it rang. Most of the time, the house was deserted until Pratap came back in the evening, completely drunk and out of his senses.

"Hello? Karthik?"

They conversed for a few minutes.

"Please, don't mention this to anyone."

Mayank stood on his feet the moment he disconnected.

Just then, he heard someone pushing the door. He got back to his wheelchair. It was Sharda with a half-burnt face.

"Ma?"

Sharda was stunned.

"Mayank, you are speaking?"

"Ma, I am normal. I can do everything. The reason I was like that was to save myself."

He told everything about how his father had strangled his own brother and that he had seen that. Just then, he pushed him from the stairs and pretended to be paralysed to save himself.

"Ma, I know where Didi is."

Pratap was standing behind, drunk, and heard everything.

"Tell me, you son of a bitch. Where is that whore?"

He tortured both of them until that fine day, Mayank gathered all his strength and stabbed Pratap while he was trying to strangle Sharda. Sharda mourned for all the pain he caused them, how her son was bound to pretend to be in a wheelchair just to save his life. He took almost two years to tell her mother about his reality.

"Why?" she screamed.

She should have supported poor Unnati after her father's death. She should not have listened to her vile husband.

"Why are women taught to follow and accept what their husbands say and want to? Oh, God!"

She pulled her own hair as she considered her to be eviler than her husband. She could have prevented this fall of her family. Poor Unnati.

****

Unnati was all over the news channels. This year's best-selling music video was hers. All cassettes and CDs were available for purchase. She was this year's Nayaka. When her face appeared on all the news channels, his sons embraced her with pride. It was time to rejoice.

"Never forget your past and where you came from, but just as your past does not describe you, your present is not the ultimate reality," it is said.

She took twelve rupees from her purse and gave it to her children, telling them to get the cassettes filled with her songs. She had just sung her sixth song, and the cassettes were filled with Rs. 2 per song by a local shopkeeper.

ACKNOWLEDGEMENTS

I sincerely thank my publisher, Inkfeathers; my father, Mr. Shachender Mohan Kaura; my father-in-law, Mr. Ashwani K. Bakshi; my mother, Mrs. Meenakshi Kaura; my mother-in-law, Mrs. Geeta Bakshi; my brother, Mr. Nitin Kaura (my true and only confidant); and my husband, Mr. Raunaq Bakshi, for their contributions to this book. These people are always present, whether they are reading my work or not, and they cheer me up even when I am not a writer or author.

Thanks to Rajeev Patel for always standing by me and guiding me throughout the writing process and book development.

Hope you'll enjoy reading the book.

ABOUT THE AUTHOR

Geetika is currently employed in an African mission in New Delhi. She is a French language trainer. A blogger on renowned pages like Youth Ki Awaaz, Womensweb, TOI, Momspresso, she has written her first solo book named "Ibiza: Love in Words." This is her second book. Mostly, she writes from real-life experiences and stories, and amalgamates them with a pinch of fiction to invoke readers' interest in gaining sensitivity towards the topic as well as to give them an unstoppable read. You can connect with her at geetikak1311@gmail.com.

INKFEATHERS PUBLISHING

India's Most Author Friendly Publishing House

Stay updated about the latest books, anthologies, events, exclusive offers, contests, product giveaways and other things that we do to support authors.

 Inkfeathers Publishing

 @InkfeathersPublishing

 @_Inkfeathers

 @Inkfeathers

 Inkfeathers.com

We'd love to connect with you!